"It's no one's fault." Her voice sounded raw with emotion. "Sara's death was an accident. I finally get that." She rushed forward and wrapped her arms around him.

His shoulders shook, but he held on tight to the lifeline she offered. She didn't know how long they stood there crying. Sinclair's arms around her made her feel safe, like the strong ties of docking rope that gave a ship stability in a storm.

The party blared in the background. She could hear laughter and music, but both were muffled by Sinclair's warm shoulder. Then the band played a slow song she remembered from high school dances.

She'd always lingered on the bleachers, wishing…

"Dance with me," he said.

Hope swallowed sudden panic.

But he gave her a hint of a smile and brushed her cheek with his thumb. "Have I ever told you that you're beautiful? Because you are, Hope, inside and out."

Books by Jenna Mindel

Love Inspired

Mending Fences
Season of Dreams
Courting Hope

JENNA MINDEL

lives in Northern Michigan with her husband, Steve, their two dogs and one sassy guinea pig named Aunt Bea. She enjoys a career in banking that has spanned over twenty-five years and several positions, but writing is her passion. A 2006 Romance Writers of America RITA® finalist, Jenna has answered her heart's call to write inspirational romances set near the Great Lakes.

Courting Hope
Jenna Mindel

Recycling programs
for this product may
not exist in your area.

™ LOVE INSPIRED BOOKS

ISBN-13: 978-0-373-81699-6

COURTING HOPE

Copyright © 2013 by Jenna Mindel

www.LoveInspiredBooks.com

Printed in U.S.A.

There is a time for everything and a season for every activity under heaven. He has made everything beautiful in its time…

—*Ecclesiastes* 3:1, 11

To EEC's very first coed softball team
and our glorious 1-13 season!
What we didn't win in games, we won in fun!

Acknowledgments:

I'd like to thank Pastor Mark and Tanya Drinkall
for sharing with me their journey and calling
into the ministry. You guys are awesome!

To my agent, Karen Solem,
for not giving up on me.
And my editor, Melissa Endlich,
for giving me another wonderful opportunity
to write for Love Inspired. Thank you both!

Chapter One

Mondays were Hope Petersen's favorite day. They were quiet days. Mondays helped her forget Sundays, where the family dinner table reminded her of the one person no longer there.

Hope stopped typing to stare out the window of her small office in the lower level of Three Corner Community Church. It'd been almost three years since Sara had died, and she could hear her sister's voice telling her to get over it already. To move on. Stop trying to fix Mom and Dad and get a boyfriend.

"Fat chance," Hope muttered.

Working in a small church consumed her time and kept her anchored to the northern Michigan farm community where she'd grown up. It wasn't easy meeting the right kind of guy.

Hope turned her focus back to updating the church website with the previous Sunday's sermon. Delivered by an elder on the board who was filling in until they hired a permanent minister, the notes were pretty short. And dull, from the looks of them. She was glad she'd missed it.

"Hello, Hope."

She knew that deep voice despite not having heard it in years. Hating the shiver that raced through her, Hope balled her hands into fists and looked up.

Sinclair Marsh stood in the doorway of the office, waiting for her response. His mouth lifted into the boyishly crooked smile she remembered well. That smile had always landed him whatever he wanted. That same smile had enticed Sara to follow his reckless, Pied Piper path to her death.

He'd aged. Could be the dark-rimmed glasses he now wore, which made his hazel eyes look like they'd seen too much. It didn't matter. His simple words of greeting turned her inside out.

"What are you doing here?" Hope's thick voice came out in a rough whisper.

"You don't know?"

"Know what?" Her voice grew stronger even though her throat threatened to close up. The church board had been interviewing for months. Surely they hadn't made their decision while she was gone.

"I'm the new pastor."

Hope clenched her teeth to keep from saying

something she shouldn't. Too many descriptions came to mind when she thought of Sin Marsh, and *pastor* wasn't one of them.

He shifted his stance to make room for Judy Graves. Judy was an elder and longtime member of the church board. The backbone of the church, Judy was their financial guru as well as head of the volunteer program. And Judy happened to be best friends with Hope's mom.

Hope looked toward Judy. She wanted answers. "I thought you were going with someone named Smythe."

"I'm plan B." Sinclair stepped forward as if reminding her of his presence.

As if she'd forget. Why hadn't they told her?

Judy stared her down, sending strong messages of her own. "I'm giving *Pastor Sinclair* the tour. He'll need to see the year-to-date financials, as well as go over day-to-day stuff. I'm going to show him his office so he can get settled in, but I'll be back."

With a gaping mouth, Hope watched the two of them leave. Well, her Monday was officially shot! Thoughts spinning, she gulped for air, but the June breeze coming in through the open window wasn't enough. Suffocation was eminent if she didn't hightail her way out of there.

Grabbing her purse, Hope headed for her car. She tossed her purse on the passenger seat but didn't climb in. The wind ruffled her short hair and swirled the folds of her long gauzy skirt against her legs.

Of all the men they could have hired, why Sinclair Marsh? Since when had he come home?

She stared at the ripe hayfields across the road until her vision blurred with memories. Not quite three years ago, her dad's hayfield had needed its final cut. Hope could smell the sweetness of freshly cut hay—could almost taste the dust kicked up from the tractor. Sara's laughter rolled through her memory, too. Sara had been so full of laughter.

Hope was supposed to help her sister with that cut, but she'd gone shopping instead for her planned trip to Spain. Hope had landed a job with a worldwide missions organization and could hardly wait to leave.

Besides, Ryan Marsh was Sara's fiancé and he and Sinclair had come over to lend a hand. Like always, they'd goofed around. Only this time, their antics had ended with Sara dead—crushed under the tractor after it had flipped. Sinclair had mowed a patch of grass into the letter *S* on the side of a hill, and he'd dared Sara to do the same....

Hope heard footsteps on the tarmac, but she didn't turn around. If it was Sinclair, she might just let him have it.

"You okay?" Judy touched her shoulder.

She flinched. "I can't work here."

"I had a feeling you might react this way."

Hope whirled around and slammed her car door. "But you hired him anyway!"

"It wasn't my decision alone. We interviewed him last week, and the board unanimously approved Sinclair after Reverend Smythe took a position downstate."

Hope reveled in the satisfaction that for once, Sinclair had come in second place. But the smug feeling was short lived. "Why didn't you call me?"

"You were on vacation. I love your new hairstyle, by the way."

Hope shrugged off the compliment. She would have liked to have known about Sinclair. She'd have had time to prepare instead of seeing him out of the blue like this.

Even though she'd grown up with Sinclair and they'd hung around like pals, Hope had never felt comfortable around guys. Growing up with a mouth full of braces and a chest a tad too big made her want to hide. And hide she did—under clothes, hair…even her eyeglasses gave her a sense of protection.

Not anymore. She'd long since gotten rid of the baggy clothes and glasses, and thanks to the prodding of a girlfriend from college, Hope had finally cut her mop of hair. The two of them had spent last week in Toronto shopping and taking in shows.

Hope shifted her stance, wishing she could find a way to hide again. "I'm not going back in there. You're going to have to find somebody else."

Judy's eyes narrowed. "What about the school?"

For years the church had raised money to build an addition for a couple of *real* classrooms. The extra space would accommodate Sunday school classes and enable them to start a small preschool during the week. Hope also wanted to include a summer program. Too many single moms in the church had too few options during the summer months.

Hope had a dual degree in early education and Spanish. She'd been dreaming about running the educational interests of the church for as long as she could remember. As part of the building project committee, she'd researched state licensing requirements, commercial financing and local builders. The church had been poised to accept bids for construction once the pledges were paid. And then their previous minister had retired early due to health concerns and moved away.

Interim pastors and a wavering church body had stalled the plan. They needed the right man leading the charge to get the project back on track. Sinclair Marsh could *not* be that man.

"Without you, that school doesn't stand a chance."

Hope lifted her chin. "The groundwork's all there."

Judy scanned the surrounding fields before focusing back on her. "Sinclair has a new idea that's less costly. Some of the board members like it. A lot."

"What kind of new idea?" Hope could only imagine the irresponsible suggestions Sinclair might have.

"A youth center, Hope. He'd like to propose a place for teens to hang out and stay away from trouble."

"Out here?" Hope sputtered. Had they been in town, she could see the need for something like that. But they were a few miles out. Fruit farms dotted the hills and valleys between older homes, and new subdivisions had been halted because of the downturn in the economy. "That's a stupid idea."

"Well, it's an idea that struck a chord with the board, especially Chuck. We need you here, Hope. I need you."

She looked into Judy's earnest gaze, knowing she was sunk. Hope had promised her friend Dorrie that she'd never give up on the preschool, and yet here she was, ready to quit. All because of Sinclair Marsh.

Swallowing hard, Hope thought about another issue. "What about Mom and Dad?"

"I believe with all my heart that God wants Sinclair to lead our church. I can't say I know why, but it feels right. Maybe in time we'll figure that out, but right now I pray your parents will give him a chance. I want you to do that, too."

"I can't." Her eyes blurred again. "Not after what happened."

Judy pulled her into a warm embrace. "No matter the influence, your sister was an adult who made her own choice to do something foolish. I know you miss her, Hope, but harboring unforgiveness toward Sinclair isn't good for you. It isn't good for anyone."

She shook her head against Judy's strong shoulder. As far as Hope was concerned, Sinclair was the reason she no longer had a sister.

"You've got to let it go."

Hope pulled out of the older woman's embrace. "How? There isn't a day that goes by that feels right. Dad misses Sara. I can see it in his eyes. It's like I'm left with clouds and can't make the sun shine again."

"It's not up to you to make the sun shine for them. They have to find that sunshine on their own." Judy squeezed her shoulder. "You think about that school. You have a calling for it. Can you really walk away?"

Hope sucked in her bottom lip. Judy knew the right buttons to push. God could work it all out, but what if quitting messed up His plan?

A youth center? Hope had talked Sinclair out of

his set course several times when they were kids. Could she do it again?

Judy gave her shoulder a gentle squeeze. "Come back when you're ready."

Hope watched her mother's lifelong friend walk away, knowing Judy was right. If she quit now, what chance did Hope have for getting the preschool project back on track? It'd fizzle and die—another dream gone.

An image of the completed addition blazed through her mind. Dorrie and her two girls were part of that image. They needed supervision over the summer break. Lots of kids did. Hope knew the community and its needs. Unfortunately, so did Sinclair. After all, he was a local boy returned home.

Tipping her head back with a groan, Hope stared at the blue sky above. Like it or not, people depended on her and she needed to get back to work.

Sinclair took in the small space of his barren office. He had a desk, a couple chairs and a bookshelf. He could easily see Hope's empty desk from his. The church offices had been situated along the side of the basement opposite the kitchen and an open area used for Sunday school and probably fellowship dinners. He had a nice-sized window with a view of hayfields, and beyond the parking lot, cherry orchards covered the hills and more fields.

He spotted Hope pacing. She'd changed since the last time he'd seen her. A family member's death did that to a person on some level, but he also detected a confidence in her that he didn't remember. Her outward appearance was different, too—so different, it had taken him a couple minutes to recognize her.

Hope had slimmed down, losing her college freshman fifteen and then some. With her bushy long hair cut into a short cap of dusky waves, she looked good. Maybe too good. And they'd be working together.

He'd searched online for ministry positions in northern Michigan for months. There were three churches in his hometown of LeNaro, but the only pastoral staff opening had been here—a community church three miles north of town and smack in the middle of cherry farm country.

He should have known that Hope might still work in this office. She'd worked here through college, but she'd been planning to go to Spain the summer he'd left. He never thought to ask about her during his interview.

He stepped away from the window. Knowing Hope ran the office wouldn't have made a lick of difference in his decision. He'd come home to make amends for his past. If he faced an uphill battle, it was no less than he deserved.

His brother Ryan barely spoke to him, and Hope still blamed him for Sara's death. He could see it in her eyes. Her pretty gray eyes that were no longer hidden behind Coke-bottle glasses.

Judy stuck her head into his office. "You okay?"

He nodded, even though it felt like he'd been hit in the gut by a ground ball that had taken a bad hop. "I take it Jim and Teresa Petersen attend here, as well. Maybe I should call and let them know."

It was his first position as a pastor, and he'd walked into a personal beehive. He could take getting stung, but for how long?

"I'll talk to them tonight and let you know how it goes." Judy's eyes softened.

"Thanks."

Three years ago, Judy Graves had encouraged him to work through Sara's accident by sticking around to face his part in it. Judy had been firmly in his corner during the short police investigation. It looked like she was still there.

"You're here for a reason, Sinclair. Don't forget that."

"It's why I came home."

Judy gave him a thatta-boy nod and left.

Sinclair glanced back at the window, where sunlight streamed into the room. He stood and opened it, letting in a cool breeze despite the uncommonly hot weather for mid-June in northern Michigan. He'd never grown accustomed to the oppressive heat he'd experienced in the years he spent in Haiti, but he'd managed. He'd worked through it. He'd do the same with Hope, if she'd let him.

Hope wiped her face with fast-food napkins that she had stashed in her car's glove compartment before stepping out of her Jetta. After a therapeutic cry and some soft music, she felt halfway ready to go back to work.

She spotted Sinclair reaching into an ancient candy-apple-red Camaro. He still drove that target for speeding tickets. He hadn't changed.

"Nice image for a minister."

He whirled around and smiled. "What?"

It was a cruel joke that a guy nicknamed Sin had such a tempting smile. She'd always called him by his full name. Not only did she like it better, but she believed using his full name shielded her from the temptation to follow his antics into trouble.

Sometimes it had worked. Sometimes it hadn't.

She pointed at his vehicle. "That car."

His smile only grew wider. "I'm not about an image."

Hope gave a snort and lifted one eyebrow.

Who was he trying to kid? He reeked with the same reckless charm he'd always had. All show and no substance, like the ridiculously fast car he'd driven since high school.

"That car will do you no good come winter, you know." Hope sounded like somebody's mother. No, worse, someone's grandmother.

Sinclair's smile widened. "I know. I'll figure it out."

He was good at doing that. He constantly lived with a no worries now, figure it out later mentality. She remembered a youth rally they'd attended, and Sinclair had confided in her that he'd been called to the ministry. He'd bragged to her that he'd pastor a church someday, but she'd laughed at the idea. Hope hadn't believed he'd follow through. Yet here he was, her new pastor.

He walked toward her. "I'm worried you might quit."

"I might."

"Please don't."

"Why?" Hope enjoyed watching him squirm for an answer.

Then he looked at her with intense eyes and said, "Because I need you."

How many years had she dreamed of hearing those words come from him? Hope swallowed hard and looked away. Sinclair Marsh never needed anyone.

"That bothers you." His voice was laced with empathy.

"*You* bother me." Hope didn't want his understanding. She didn't want anything from him anymore.

"I'm sorry to hear that." His voice softened.

Was that regret she read in his eyes? She quickly looked away again. "How 'bout you do your job, and I'll do mine."

"Our jobs cross. We're going to end up in the middle of that intersection quite a bit. What then?"

He made a good point. How in the world were they going to go about their day-to-day duties without crashing into each other? "We'll just have to deal with it."

His gaze softened further. "Hope—"

She held her hand up to stop him from talking about Sara. "Don't go there."

"We have to. Eventually."

"Maybe, but not today." Hope turned and headed for the church office.

By the time Hope made it home later that afternoon, her emotions were all over the place. She felt rubbed raw. All afternoon she'd been aware of Sinclair's presence. At the coffeemaker or the laser printer. The last straw had been hearing him on the piano upstairs in the sanctuary. The guy had played heart-wrenchingly beautiful music for a solid hour. By four o'clock, she couldn't take it anymore and left work half an hour early.

Sitting in the driveway, Hope hesitated before getting out of her car. Looking at the white farmhouse where she'd grown up and still called home at the ripe age of twenty-seven, Hope wondered how she'd break the news of their new minister to her folks.

With a sigh, she got out and trudged toward the house. Her mother met her at the side door, letting out their black-and-white shepherd mix named Gypsy. "Judy called."

Hope cringed. Did they already know? "What did she want?"

"Why didn't you tell us the church hired Sinclair Marsh?"

"Because I just found out today."

"Why didn't they bring you in on the decision?"

Hope let her head fall back. "I don't know, Mom. I was on vacation. Besides, the board found interim pastors without my input, so I guess they didn't need it. Can we talk about this later? I'm beat."

"Your father's not happy."

Hope didn't expect that he would be.

"I think you should talk to him." Her mom gave her a ghost of a smile.

She didn't feel encouraged. "Now?"

"He's in the barn."

Hope left her purse on the bench against the wall in the kitchen before she plodded back down the porch steps. They had a small farm with a whole lot of cattle for beef. An oddity, considering the surrounding fruit growers. Entering the barn, she spotted her father in his workshop with a blowtorch and soldering wire.

She slipped into a nearby chair and waited. It didn't take long for one of the barn cats to find its way onto her lap.

When her dad finished mending the metal, he flipped up his safety glasses and looked at her. His eyes were red. Could be from the work, or something else?

"Hi, Daddy."

"You gonna quit?"

"No." She stroked the calico cat's fur. How could she?

"Don't expect us to go there." Her father slipped his glasses back in place. Conversation over.

Hope watched her father finish fixing whatever it was for one of the tractor engines. He had kept the tractor that had crushed Sara. Her father's rationale had been that it wasn't the tractor's fault it flipped.

True. It was Sinclair's. And Hope's for not being

there to stop her sister from doing something so stupid.

Hope often wondered if it would have been easier on her dad if she had been the one under that tractor. Sara had been his kindred spirit—the one who wanted to take over the farm someday. Sara had been the one who knew how to help. Her little sister didn't need to be told what needed to be done or shown how to do it. Sara just knew.

Hope didn't know. She'd tried, but she couldn't fill the empty void Sara left behind.

"Put those in the box over there, would you?" Her father handed her his safety glasses.

Hope gently shooed the cat down and brushed off her skirt. She laid the glasses alongside a few other pairs and closed the lid, careful to keep the edge of her skirt from brushing the greasy side of the workbench.

"You should have changed your clothes before coming out here."

Hope shrugged. "It's okay."

"Your mother sent you, didn't she?"

Hope nodded.

"We were finally getting some distance." Her father's face looked worn.

"I know." Her heart tore in two. They may have accepted Sara's death, but Sinclair's return reopened the wound and made it feel fresh and sore, like a torn scab.

"Let's see what your mother has cooked up, huh?"

Hope followed her father out of his workshop. The dog flew past them, barking the whole way, toward a candy-apple-red Camaro that pulled into the driveway.

Sinclair.

"What's he want?" her father growled.

"I'll send him on his way." She glanced into her father's metal-gray eyes, which looked hard as steel.

Her father slowed her down with a touch of his hand. "Wait. I want to hear what he's come to say."

Hope focused on Sinclair as he made his way toward them up the long gravel drive. What did he think he was doing here? The dog trotted alongside him with her tail wagging. Gypsy had always loved Sinclair. Everyone had loved Sinclair.

Once upon a time, Hope had, too.

"Gypsy, come!" She grabbed the dog's collar and put her in the house.

"Who's here?" Her mother stepped onto the porch, wiping her hands on a dish towel.

"Sinclair Marsh," Hope answered, then watched her mother's expression change to tense concern.

When Sinclair stopped near the porch, the air turned thick and heavy with emotion. There were things that had never been said. Forgiveness that was never granted.

Hope would never forget that day she'd returned

from shopping to the horrible scene enfolding in the living room. The police had asked Ryan questions while her father had tried to console her mother. Sinclair had stood alone, looking pale and guilty.

This wasn't going to go well.

"Mr. and Mrs. Petersen. I didn't call first, because I figured I should say this in person." Sinclair looked directly at her father.

"Say what?" her father asked with impatience.

Her mother stepped down to stand next to her husband in the driveway. They'd always thought Sinclair irresponsible. They used to tell her he was a young man they couldn't trust. Seeing them standing so stiff, the two reminded Hope of a stone wall. Like a permanent fixture of the landscape, her parents were bound to be hard to move.

Hope stayed on the porch and watched and waited.

"I wanted to let you know that I'm the new pastor at Three Corner Community Church."

"We heard."

"And…I'm sorry." Sinclair didn't waver in his stance. He met her parents' stone-cold stares without flinching.

"Three years and you're sorry." Her father's voice was low with sarcasm and hurt.

Hope noticed the skin on Sinclair's neck flush red. This wasn't easy for him, either.

"I can't change what happened or my part in it. But I wanted you both to know—" he glanced at her "—the three of you to know, that I'm done running from it."

Hope watched her father. He looked like a tractor that had been worked too hard and might blow a gasket. And yet Sinclair hadn't looked away. He faced them with an honest humility she'd never seen in him before. There was no sense of challenge in him, no cockiness.

"That's what you've come to say?"

Sinclair gave a quick nod. "That's it."

"Okay then, you've said it." Her father stuffed his hands in his pockets. Conversation over.

Only Sinclair didn't take the cue right away. He looked like he might say something else but thought better of it. With a tight upper lip, he gave her mother another stiff nod. "Good night, then."

The three of them watched in silence as Sinclair walked down the drive, got back into his car and pulled out.

Hope released the breath she'd been holding. Not nearly as bad as she'd thought.

"Hope, if you were smart, you'd rethink working there." Her father stomped up the stairs and entered the house.

Hope didn't move. She didn't speak, either. She might say something she'd regret. It didn't matter that she'd felt the same way today; she was tired of orders and expectations.

She was too old to still live at home, but how could she leave her folks? Her father refused to talk about what had happened, and her mom did her best to keep things even-keeled. And Hope got lost in the mix of trying to please them.

Glancing at the dozen flowerpots she'd helped her mother fill with red geraniums, Hope opened the screen door and went inside. The door closed with a snap behind her.

Her mom caressed her shoulder and smiled. "Give him time, Hope."

Time? They'd been doing this agonizing dance for too long. She silently followed her mother to the kitchen sink to wash her hands for dinner. No matter how much it might hurt her parents, Hope wasn't about to quit. Not when the preschool hung in the balance. She'd walked away from so much in her short life, she couldn't walk away from that. Not without a fight.

Chapter Two

The next morning, Sinclair rushed through the office entrance. He had a box of his sister's cherry almond scones ready for a peace offering. He glanced at the clock on the wall and grimaced. Nine-thirty. He'd wanted to make it in by nine.

Hope stood near the coffeemaker, looking pretty in a filmy blue top over a white skirt that kissed her knees. The girl he remembered wore shapeless clothes that hid everything. Part of him wished for the old Hope who didn't have this power to distract him.

He stepped forward, but kept his voice soft. "Morning, Hope."

She finished stirring creamer into her coffee before turning to glare at him. "How could you do that?"

He didn't bother with the pretense of asking what she meant. He knew. "I had to face them."

"Did you really? On your first day? You couldn't let Judy's news sink in a little and give them a chance to process it?"

"They deserved to hear it from me."

"So you go on a search-and-destroy mission to make the Petersens bleed all over again?"

He set the box of scones on her desk. Did he get it all wrong? He'd prayed so hard before making the decision to go to Hope's house. He'd wanted to clear the air and offer his remorse. Show them that he meant business and was serious about his calling. Looked like he'd botched it. "I'm sorry."

She made a rude sound. She'd always been able to make him feel like an idiot.

"I'm trying to do the right thing here."

Her shoulders drooped and all the fight blew out of her as quickly as it had raged. "I wish I knew what that was."

He stepped forward to touch her shoulder, but he let his hand drop to his side instead. He'd lost the right to offer her comfort when he'd lost her as a friend. When Sara had died.

"They want me to quit."

"Your parents?" Of course that's who she was talking about.

She nodded but wouldn't look at him.

He'd seen a glimmer of softening in Teresa Petersen's eyes last night. There was hope for forgiveness yet. But he couldn't rush. That had always been his problem. He rushed too much.

"You still do everything your parents want you to?" He didn't mean to lower his voice, but his challenge came across pretty clear if the scowl on Hope's face was any indication.

She still toed the family line. Always responsible, Hope had a servant's heart that could be taken advantage of. Sinclair regretted that he'd been on the using end far too many times in the past. He remembered calling on Hope for a ride home after he'd partied too hard on summer break. He'd even asked her to pick out Christmas gifts for his mom and sister a couple years in a row. And she'd done what he'd asked because she was a giver instead of a taker like him.

She looked at him with wide eyes. "Who do you think you are?"

The blue of her top made her eyes an icy gray color that looked translucent. Protective and fierce. Sinclair couldn't look away.

The phone rang, interrupting the moment, but he ignored it. He remained focused on her. "I've known you longer than I haven't."

"You don't know anything." She reached for the phone. "Three Corner Community Church, how may I help you?"

He watched the graceful way she cradled the receiver between her chin and shoulder while she grabbed a pad of paper and a pen. He didn't know this new Hope who appeared completely in charge. The urge to get to know her on a very personal level took him by surprise. He didn't want this attraction to Hope. It complicated everything—but what could he do?

"Yeah, he's right here." Hope caught him staring and her cheeks colored. "It's Judy. She's headed out of town for a couple of days and wants to know if you need anything before she goes. You can take it in your office."

"Here's fine." He sat on the edge of her desk and reached for the phone.

Hope gave him a pointed look. She wasn't handing over the call until he moved off of her desk.

Without looking away, he slipped from the edge and accepted the phone. "Hey, Judy…"

Hope peeked inside the box of scones and smiled. Finally, a glimpse of his old Hope.

Reassuring Judy that he'd get the budget and building plans, he cut the conversation short. "I'll be fine. Thanks. Have a safe trip."

He leaned forward, catching a whiff of Hope's flowery perfume as he hung up. "I know you like scones."

Hope looked annoyed. Obviously pointing out her weakness for baked goods hadn't scored him any points. She grabbed a scone and then pushed the box toward him.

"They're from my sister."

"How is Eva?" Hope took a bite.

"Engaged."

Hope headed for the coffee station and grabbed a napkin. "Good for her. I didn't see anything in the paper."

"It's pretty recent. She's marrying the guy who bought the orchard." Sinclair followed her and helped himself to coffee.

"I'd heard that your parents sold and moved. How are they?"

"Here for the summer to help bring in what's left of the harvest." He'd returned home after severe thunderstorms had ripped through area orchards. His sister was determined to salvage a decent crop, and he'd do what he could to help.

Hope nodded. "They must be glad you're home."

"Yeah." He bit into a scone, but the flavor was lost when he thought of his brother's cold reception. His family had eagerly welcomed him, but not Ryan. More amends to be made. Sara Petersen had been Ryan's fiancée.

"Well, thank you for these." Hope settled into her office chair with a look that said she was determined to get back to work.

Sinclair didn't want their conversation to end. He used to pour his heart out to her when they were kids. Breakups with girlfriends, trouble with his father, dreams about his future. He used to tell Hope everything. Back then, she'd been more than a sympathetic listener. More times than not, she'd tell him flat out that he was wrong and make him see the other side. She gave him balance.

He didn't feel too balanced around her today. Giving her his best pleading look, he asked, "Does this mean you're not going to quit?"

Hope stared into Sinclair's eyes and didn't answer right away. She liked holding her employment future over his head. Even though she'd never quit, she wanted to punish him. As if it'd matter.

She hadn't counted on the intensity shining from his eyes and wished he'd go away already. "Not today."

He looked relieved. Sinclair needed her to stay. He needed *her*.

She didn't care for the fleeting warmth that swirled through her at the thought. Not one bit.

He returned to the corner of her desk. "What are you working on?"

She gave him her most intimidating glare, but he stayed put. "I'm updating our website with your bio as the new pastor."

"Where'd you get the information?"

Hope kept typing. If she ignored him, maybe he'd go away. "From your résumé."

"Keep it short and to the point, okay?"

Hope looked up at him then. "You want to proof this?"

"No."

"Fine." Hope waited for him to leave.

"Okay then, good." He pushed his glasses up the bridge of his nose. "We should probably have a staff meeting this week. There's a receptionist, right? And a janitor?"

"Both are part-time. Shannon Williams works a few hours a day and covers lunch hour phones, but her baby was sick yesterday. She and her husband also volunteer their time with the youth. Walt comes in the afternoon since he works another job in the morning. And Judy's here every morning. But then, you probably already know that since she's on the board and interviewed you. We're a big ol' staff of five, not including you."

"You know everyone's schedule better than I do. Let me know when you want to meet."

Hope bit her lip. She'd always scheduled meetings for her previous pastor, but it wasn't easy taking direction from Sinclair. Hope was too used to telling him no.

When they were kids, he used to egg her on to do things she knew better than to do. Like when she was fourteen and they'd jumped off the LeNaro Bridge with inner tubes to float down the river. She'd split her lip on the air stem. Hope fingered the now tiny scar. Her parents had pitched a fit because she'd needed five stitches.

The word *no* hung on the tip of her tongue.

"Problem?" He waited for her acquiescence.

Hope came back to the present. "Nope. I'll let you know by the end of today."

He finally slipped off her desk. "Good. Can I review the annual budget and the financial report for the building project?"

"I'll email them to you." Hope shoved a slip of paper his way. "This is your church email. I'll also set up a shared calendar schedule that we can both access."

"Cool." His finger touched hers as he tried to grab the note.

Hope quickly pulled her hand back. The phone rang again, shattering the awareness that tingled through her. Answering on the second ring, she breathed easier when Sinclair walked toward his own office.

"I'm sorry, Mrs. Larson, what was that?" Hope hadn't heard a word.

While she chatted about dessert possibilities to welcome Sinclair after Wednesday night's service, Shannon slipped into the receptionist desk. She gave Hope a wave and craned her neck to get a peek at their new pastor.

Finally off the phone, Hope jotted down her to-do list for tomorrow's errands. She'd have Walt set up a couple of tables at the back of the sanctuary for refreshments, and she'd pick up cookies from the bakery in town. Mrs. Larson would see to the punch. They already had a supply of cups and napkins in the church kitchen.

"Wow, Hope. He's cute." Shannon had been trying to fix her up since they'd met. "Is he single?"

Hope shrugged. "He's not married."

"Girlfriend?"

"I don't know." Hope didn't care to know. Really, she didn't.

"We'll have to find out." Shannon stood. "Come on, introduce me."

Again, Hope shook her head. "Look, I grew up with him. I'm not interested, so you can forget whatever you're thinking."

Shannon looked at Sinclair and then at her. "Hmm. So you two have a history. This should be very interesting!"

The next day, Sinclair slumped in the kitchen after polishing off an evening snack. The house belonged to his sister, Eva, now, and she shared the place with her friend Beth. And his parents were staying through the summer. It was pretty spacious for an old farmhouse, but felt cramped. Sinclair wanted a place of his own. He needed to be by himself. After three years of living in crowded staff quarters for the orphanage school in Haiti, Sinclair longed for quiet. When things settled down, he'd look for something.

He ran his thumbnail along a groove in the old oak kitchen table where he'd eaten hundreds of meals as a kid. Meeting the congregation had not gone as planned. They seemed like a warm group of people. But after his message had landed with a wet-bag-of-cement thud, he wondered if he'd gotten his calling all wrong.

"You look tired, Sinclair. How was your first midweek service?" His mom rubbed his shoulders.

He was glad his parents hadn't been there to witness his failure. "I've had better."

"Want to talk about it?"

He shrugged.

His staff didn't take him seriously. Hope spoke to him only when necessary, and Shannon, the receptionist, acted like she knew something he didn't. Walt, the maintenance guy, thought he was too young, and tonight he'd blown his first message delivered from the pulpit. Three days into his first week as a pastor, and the job was nothing like he'd expected.

Wednesday night services were less formal than Sunday, so he'd thought he could be more…honest. He'd definitely made an impression, but if the blank stares were any indication, not the kind he'd wanted.

Had his congregation missed the whole point of his tales of Haiti? He might have driven it home too hard that they had so much while the people he'd served in Haiti had next to nothing. He'd probably been too graphic, but folks should know the truth.

With a sigh, he confessed, "I think I shocked a few people tonight."

Rose Marsh slid into the seat across from him. "Maybe they need to be shocked. It's never a good thing to get too comfortable in the pew."

He smiled at his mom. At only five foot two, she was a powerhouse of opinion who didn't believe in beating around the bush. She didn't stand for sulking, either. "Maybe you're right."

"You know I am." His mom flashed him a cocky grin. "I understand Hope Petersen works with you."

Sinclair lifted an eyebrow. He hadn't told anyone in his family. "How do you know?"

"Judy Graves. I ran into her at the grocery store earlier this week. How's that going?"

He shrugged again. Hope did her job well. At the welcome reception for him after the service, people had swarmed around her. She had that effect on him, too—drawing his attention like a honeybee to its hive.

"Sinclair?" His mom had an amused look on her face.

"It's a little rough around the edges, but we'll work through it."

"Maybe you should bring her to Adam and Eva's engagement party."

As if she'd go. "I don't think so."

His mom leaned forward. "She used to have quite a crush on you, you know."

That was news to him. Hope used to laugh at his many breakups with girls and say she wouldn't wish him on her worst enemy. "Hope? No way. I drove her nuts. Besides, Ryan might have a hard time with that. Too many memories."

His mom grasped his hand. "It might be good for Ryan to see Hope. It's time he moved on. Sara's been gone a long time now."

Sinclair understood why his brother had shut down. He functioned like part of him was missing—his better half. Sara Petersen had been a lighthearted soul who looked for fun in everything she did. From the time they were teens in the same youth group, Sara had drawn out his serious younger brother and made Ryan laugh like no one else could. The two had dated for years. When she'd died they were engaged, but they might as well have been married. They'd been inseparable.

"I don't know, Mom. I can't even talk to him anymore."

She patted his hand. "You weren't here when he needed you, son. Ryan won't let that go."

"Why can't he see that I was needed in Haiti, especially after the earthquake?" Sinclair had run away by going on a church mission trip a week after Sara's funeral. Once he'd been in Haiti and seen the needs of the orphanage school, he'd stayed. Ryan hadn't forgiven him for it.

"Don't give up on him. Ryan needs you even if he won't admit it. God has brought you home where you belong, Sinclair. Just hang in there."

"Thanks, Mom."

He didn't feel like he belonged here, not in his childhood home at least. God had brought him back, that much he knew. But the time spent in Haiti, coupled with the reason he'd gone there, made it hard to feel comfortable anywhere.

"Hope, can you come into my office?" Sinclair looked troubled the next morning as he filled his coffee cup.

"One sec." Hope hit Save on her computer.

He returned to his office, which was across a small corridor. Hope could see him from her desk, and she'd caught his eye several times that week without meaning to.

Sinclair had given her an interesting sermon to outline for Sunday. He wanted copies stuffed into the bulletins passed out before the service. So far, she was impressed by his preparation. Sinclair must have finally left behind his bad habit of procrastinating on studying until the last minute.

Shannon wiggled her eyebrows. "Sounds serious."

"Please stop." Hope stood and headed for the pastoral office.

She couldn't block the unease that crawled up her spine with each step she took. What could Sinclair want? They'd pretty much kept their distance the past few days.

Leaning against the doorway of his office, Hope forced herself to relax. "What's up?"

"Come in a minute, would you?"

Hope slipped into one of the two chairs in front of his desk and waited. His window was open and she could hear birds chirping in the crab apple tree outside. A warm breeze that smelled like summer blew in and rustled loose papers sitting on Sinclair's desk.

He gathered them up and stuffed them under the file labeled "Church Budget." A much fatter file containing all the information for the building project sat next to it.

Her preschool.

Clearing his throat, he looked at her. "I want to ask you something, but I need you to be completely honest."

"Okay." Hope waited.

He looked at her then. "Don't answer right away. Give it some thought."

She wiped her palms on her khaki skirt. "What is it?"

"This is going to sound so stupid." He ran his hand through his brown hair, which had been sun-streaked blond in places. And then he pushed his glasses up the bridge of his nose. A nervous habit he'd picked up. She'd never seen Sinclair nervous until these past few days. "I need to know, from someone whose judgment I trust..."

"Yes?" Hope leaned forward. Would he listen to her ideas for the project?

"Last night's message—what did you think?"

Hope blinked a couple times. "What?"

"The service, my stories. Did I come on too strong?"

"Hmm." Hope hadn't expected such a question. She'd never expected Sinclair's confidence to be shaken, either. And clearly he didn't feel confident. It made her want to smile. Big-time.

Instead, she stalled. "Why do you ask?"

"I got a lot of blank stares."

Hope didn't want to soothe him, but she couldn't lie, either. She'd been blown away by the harsh realities the Haitian people faced. Sinclair had been working at an orphanage that had swelled like a tidal wave after the earthquake. He'd witnessed devastation and death. Still, between the massive graves for the dead and the violent looting, she had a feeling that last night's message only scratched the surface of the horrors Sinclair had seen. Listening to him, Hope knew how easily he could have been killed. The reality of Sinclair gone forever had brought an unwanted ache deep in her chest.

She narrowed her gaze. "You didn't exaggerate?"

He shook his head.

"I think you made some people uncomfortable, and you'd better be ready to hear about it."

He nodded, but he didn't look like she'd given him the answer he'd wanted. Well, Hope wasn't about to pat him on the back for scaring her congregation with his experiences in Haiti. Sure, he'd met a lot of needs and served like any God-fearing person should, but running off to Haiti three years ago had been one of his wild-hair whims. He'd jumped at the chance for adventure. He'd jumped at the chance to run away from her, Ryan and every reminder of what had happened to Sara. He'd run away from his part in it. She wouldn't applaud that.

"You think I shouldn't have gone there."

What did he want from her? Hope shifted, but his direct gaze pinned her like a paper leaf on a classroom bulletin board. "To Haiti? Or last night's message?"

"Both."

She didn't want to answer that. She might let it slip how hard it had been for her after Sara had died. Despite blaming him, she'd needed him then. "All I know is that you've seen some crazy stuff."

"Real crazy."

By the shadows that glazed his eyes, she feared he might tell her just how crazy. Her throat dry, she whispered, "Why did you come home?"

"I couldn't keep running from what had happened. God led me home to face Ryan, your parents. Even you—especially you."

Hope took a deep breath but tears threatened. She fought the clogging of her throat. She didn't want to get into this. Not now. Not at work. "Don't."

"I won't. But eventually we have to."

Judy's words about holding on to her grudge echoed through her mind. It was easier to blame Sinclair than herself. If only Hope had been there. If only she hadn't gone shopping, Sara might still be alive.

He dipped his head to catch her attention. "Subject change?"

She sniffed. "Please."

"Tell me about this building project. Why a preschool?"

Hope couldn't lay open her dreams without figuring out where he was coming from and what he had planned. "Judy said you wanted a youth center."

"The board would like to eventually hire a youth pastor. To do that, we have to reach the teens in this area. A youth center might draw them to our church."

Hope gritted her teeth. "Shannon and her husband do a fine job with the youth."

"Yes, they do. But their time is limited. Especially with a new baby."

"The preschool has already been approved by the board."

"Before your minister retired a year ago. Things change, Hope."

Dread settled in the pit of her belly. "Are you changing the plan?"

He didn't answer right away. If they dropped the preschool, what then? There'd be no reason for her to stay. How could she face Dorrie when she'd promised to do everything she could to push the preschool through?

"Sinclair?"

"I don't know. I'm trying to figure it out. What's a little preschool going to do for this church?"

Hope felt her hackles rise, but she feared letting him know how much this *little* preschool meant to her. "It's all in that file. The preapproval for a commercial loan, the bids. Once the pledged money is collected, we should be able to break ground."

"This is old data. The preapproval expired. The circumstances changed the day your previous minister left."

"But Judy—"

"She's in favor of the preschool. Some of the other board members aren't so sure."

Hope gripped the edge of the chair. Judy hadn't described it quite that way. "Why do we need a youth pastor when we have a gracious couple who volunteer? Our teens are a very small group, and we're not even in town."

"That's true."

"The enrollment projections for a preschool were conservative, but there are a lot of young families in the area who responded favorably to sending their kids."

"There are good day cares around here."

Hope forced a deep breath. "We're talking about early education from a Christian worldview. There's a huge difference."

"I know you put a lot of work into this. You were a big part of the project committee and kept the ball rolling, from what I heard. What I don't know is why it's so important to you."

"Because I have a degree in early childhood education and I want to run that preschool." She'd let the words slip out before she could catch them.

Understanding spread across his face, but then his brow furrowed. "Makes sense."

What didn't make sense was that she'd let him know her dream before she could trust him with it. Trust was a moot point with Sinclair Marsh. He'd always done what he wanted.

A quick knock on the doorway of his office saved Sinclair from having to elaborate any further. A tall, barrel-chested man stood in the doorway.

"Hey, Chuck."

"Am I interrupting?" Chuck Stillwell, board member, large commercial cherry grower and the church's biggest financial supporter, stepped into Sinclair's office.

"Not at all. We're done here." Hope bounced out of her chair and left the room.

Sinclair watched her walk away as if she couldn't leave fast enough. Refocusing his attention on Chuck, he asked, "What can I do for you?"

Chuck closed the office door. "Do you mind?"

"Of course not." What else could he say?

"Your message was a little strong last night."

He braced himself for the complaint Hope had predicted he'd receive. "It's easy to forget how sheltered we are up here."

Chuck looped his hands around one knee and leaned back in his chair. "That's not where I was going. The truth isn't always comfortable, but sometimes it has to be said. Can I be blunt?"

Again he nodded. He wouldn't expect anything less from the guy, who was something of a blowhard.

"I know you've got a heart for missions. And that's good. But I'm interested in what goes on in *this* community, not some faraway place. I want to save you the trouble of asking me to support your school in Haiti, or any foreign missions for that matter."

Sinclair forced his mouth closed before he said something he'd regret. He had to think like a pastor now and respond the same way. In bible school, the motto had been that good pastors didn't react—they listened.

He sat a little straighter. "I hear you."

Chuck's eyes narrowed. "Hearing is fine, but doing is better. I get hit up for money all the time. I don't need my minister looking to me for a donation every time I turn around."

"Fair enough." He'd never ask the guy for a dime.

"But the idea of a youth center to bring in teens isn't bad. I'd like to get my nephew up here as soon as he graduates from bible school. He'd be a big help to you as a youth pastor."

Sinclair knew where this was going, and it registered why Chuck had pounced on his suggestion of a youth center. "What about the preschool? It's been approved before, and many, including you, have already pledged financial support."

"Until you've collected those pledges, I say we keep our options open."

Nice tangle. Sinclair could push for Hope's preschool or succumb to Chuck's pressure for a youth center to validate hiring a youth pastor—namely, Chuck's nephew.

He spotted the building project file on his desk and nearly sighed. Either way, he'd let someone down.

Chapter Three

Sunday morning, Sinclair stood by the kitchen sink with a cup of coffee in hand. Staring out at the sloping cherry orchard, he noticed that the fruit had grown since he'd come home. The straw-colored cherries were ripening, and promised an early harvest.

The trees on higher ground had been torn up by the storm that had rolled through the area, stripping many of their crop. A few random cherry clumps still hung in odd spots, making it look like a giant hand had swiped many away.

The hand of God? He didn't know.

Sinclair didn't understand why bad things happened to good people. Bad choices were one thing, and he'd made plenty. But an act of nature? How did that fit? The earthquake in Haiti that had bound him there had been so devastating and senseless. And yet he'd witnessed incredible faith through the darkest times. Reflecting on that faith had the power to humble him still.

What he faced now wasn't so bad.

He'd been up since dawn, and it was still early. No one else was awake. He'd prayed, gone over his notes and then prayed some more. The nerves hadn't gone away. This would be his first Sunday message as a pastor. He'd delivered sermons before but never with the responsibility that came with shepherding a flock. He sure hoped he got this one right.

Hearing footsteps on the side porch, he turned as the door opened. Adam Peece, Eva's fiancé, walked inside, followed by Ryan. Both were dressed for work in the field.

"Sinclair." Adam nodded. "That coffee up for grabs?"

"Help yourself." He watched his younger brother focus on retying the shoelaces of his work boots. "You guys are out early. What's up?"

"Trimming the sweet cherries in the orchard. Eva thinks we should open it for pick-your-own cherries since the entire block came through the storm perfectly."

"Need help?"

"We got it." Ryan stood tall, using his six-foot-plus height to intimidate.

Sinclair didn't look away. He might be half a head shorter at only five eleven, but Sinclair was tired of the dodge game they'd played since he'd come home. He was sick of Ryan shutting him out by keeping conversation at a minimum.

Adam stepped in. "I could use all the help I can get. If you've got time before church."

"I've got time. Give me a minute to change." Setting down his cup, Sinclair headed for the stairs.

It was barely six, and his service didn't start until ten. Sunday school classes had fallen off during the year Three Corner Community Church had gone without a permanent pastor. There was no need for him to arrive before nine. A couple hours working in the field might help him relax. Anything to stop worrying about the upcoming sermon.

Once in the orchard, the three of them split rows. Sinclair and Adam trimmed opposite ends, and Ryan took the middle. For the first half hour they worked in silence, but Sinclair recognized Adam's fervor immediately. The guy moved at a quick, efficient clip that reminded him of his dad, Bob Marsh. Except Adam looked like there was no other place he'd rather be. He even hummed as he worked.

"He really loves this." Sinclair jerked his head toward his future brother-in-law.

Ryan cracked a hint of a smile. "He's just like

Eva in that respect. They've got big plans for this place."

"Dad seems happy about it."

"He's glad to help without having the worry that goes with owning it." Ryan snipped a high branch.

Sinclair smiled. Their father had finally realized the beauty of carefree living after selling the orchard. He loved knowing that his dad was happy. He also loved having a conversation of more than five words with his brother. It might be stilted, but it was a start.

"Slow and steady." The words slipped out like a prayer.

Maybe they were his, or maybe God had put them on his tongue. Didn't matter, really. Sinclair had learned from his botched attempt to make amends with Hope and her parents. He couldn't rush forgiveness. He wanted to earn it, but he knew better. It was a gift that had to be offered. It was a gift he didn't deserve.

"What?" Ryan asked.

Sinclair shrugged. "Dad's finally free."

Ryan's eyes narrowed. "He loved this farm."

"Maybe for a time, but it was slowly choking the life out of him. Like it did to Gramps."

Their grandfather had shot himself while cleaning his gun in the pole barn. It was deemed an accident, and the life insurance money paid off the farm debts so their father inherited with a clean slate. Their grandfather had been in such deep financial trouble that Sinclair wondered if the "accident" hadn't been intentional. No one really knew.

"You never liked the orchard," Ryan's voice accused, even though the questions surrounding Gramps's fate were part of the reason Ryan never wanted to take over the orchard.

"Nope, I never did. But I can appreciate its beauty and the value of having it."

An image of Hope sitting at her desk seared his brain. He'd never before noticed her quiet beauty hidden underneath all that hair and those glasses.

They'd both played ball in high school. She'd been on the girls' softball team, while he played baseball. He'd treated her like one of the guys. They used to throw a ball back and forth and talk for hours. She'd been his friend and confidante, but he'd taken their friendship for granted.

He'd kissed her once, but it had been a joke. An impulsive stunt after a bunch of guys in youth group had dared him to ask her to go snipe hunting. The toughest nut to crack, Hope had always been sensible and smart. He thought she'd see right through his request and turn him down flat. But she didn't. She'd gone with him into the woods to look for an imaginary snipe. After pulling her close to point out a nest in a pine tree, he'd stolen a kiss.

Back then he'd laughed at her eager response, and Hope had punched his arm for it. When he'd asked her why she'd gone along with the prank, she'd given him a lame explanation about wanting the practice. She'd told him that he was the safest guy she knew to practice kissing with.

Only Sinclair couldn't remember Hope ever kissing anyone else. Or dating anyone, either. She'd gone to the prom with one of his friends, but Sinclair had put the fear of God in the guy if he so much as touched Hope the wrong way. Sinclair had her back—at least that's what he'd thought then.

The memory of her tender lips on his made him stop and think. What if his mom was right about Hope having a crush on him all those years ago? Looking at it now, he felt ashamed of how callously he'd treated her. How clueless he'd been.

What surprised him more than his mother's revelation was his interest in rekindling that part of their past. Truth be told, he wanted to kiss Hope again and see what happened.

No way would he go there, though. He had no desire to become a wedge between her and her parents. Plus, working together made dating a miry slope he shouldn't start down.

Nope, Hope was definitely better off without him trying to start something he wasn't ready to finish. She deserved more than that.

* * *

"Thanks for filling in for me, Shannon. I owe you one." Hope closed her phone and took a seat at the table for breakfast.

Gypsy lay on her bed in the corner of the kitchen, thumping her tail every now and then. The dog knew better than to beg, especially when she'd get scraps after the meal was over.

"What was that about?" her father asked.

"Shannon's going to lead children's church." Hope stabbed a couple pancakes with her fork and stacked them on her plate.

Hope wanted to hear Sinclair's first sermon. Had to, really, in case of content complaint. She'd gotten only one phone call about his Wednesday night message, but still. What if he wanted her opinion about Sunday's service? She'd have to be there to hear it.

Sipping from her glass of orange juice, she caught an exchanged glance between her mother and father. "What?"

Her mother perked up. "Does this mean you're going to go with us?"

They were following through on their threat. Her parents wouldn't attend Three Corner Church with Sinclair Marsh as pastor. "Where are you going?"

"A church in Northport," her father said between mouthfuls.

Hope knew of several. One was on the loud side, and she couldn't imagine her folks staying there, but there were other choices. Good choices. She took a deep breath and answered honestly. "I'd like to hear Sinclair's first Sunday sermon."

Her father looked ready to grumble, but her mom stopped him with a touch of her hand. "I heard he shocked quite a few with his stories of Haiti."

Hope had received only one call. "From who?"

"Mary Stillwell."

"She exaggerates." Hope spread tart cherry preserves on her pancakes before dousing them with syrup. It was something she'd learned to do from Sinclair's sister, Eva, way back when.

"You're defending him." Her father's eyes narrowed.

"All I'm saying is that he didn't sugarcoat the truth."

He used to. Sinclair could put a positive spin on anything, especially on what he wanted. A natural charmer of people, Sinclair was a leader. He'd had the makings of a fine salesman, or politician even.

Or pastor.

In a way, ministers were persuaders of the truth. And Sinclair Marsh had been the master of persuasion. Hope had the scars to prove it.

For the first time since he'd returned home, Hope found herself hoping for a little of the old

Sinclair charm when it came to this morning's service. She wanted the congregation to embrace him so he could lead the way toward getting the preschool built. Once she convinced him that it was the *right* vision for Three Corner Community Church.

"And you believe him," her dad muttered.

"Yes." Hope looked at her watch and pushed her plate of half-eaten pancakes aside. She didn't want to get into it with her parents. She'd heard him speak. They hadn't. "I've got to go."

"Leaving a bit early, don't you think?" Her mom gave her an odd look.

"I've got some stuff to do in the office." Hope hurried for the door.

She didn't want to explain that nothing specific waited for her. Hope wanted to be available before the service in case Sinclair needed information. He'd told her Friday that he wanted to give the church an update on the building project. She wasn't about to miss that.

"When will you be home?" Her mom looked concerned. Dinnertime was a big deal in the Petersen household.

"I'm not sure. I'll call if I'm late." Hope grabbed her purse, wondering for the hundredth time if it wasn't past time she moved out.

She'd traded part of her life because her folks had lost part of theirs. The part that had looked forward to Sara taking over the farm. And the part that had yearned for grandchildren from Sara and Ryan.

Glancing back at the kitchen table, her heart twisted. Her parents had aged in the past three years. They were still young, but to Hope they seemed tired. The joy in working the farm was lost.

How could she leave them?

"Bye, honey." Her mom waved.

Her father grunted something that sounded like good-bye.

Hope didn't like disappointing them, but she wasn't leaving her church with the preschool up in the air. Not when they needed her vote. She wouldn't give up because Sinclair made her folks uncomfortable. He made her uncomfortable, too, but for reasons she'd rather not examine.

When Hope pulled into the church parking lot, she immediately spotted the red Camaro. It was pretty hard to miss the car's shiny wax job. She shook her head. He'd always loved that car.

She walked toward the church but stopped when she heard the sound of music drifting out the open windows of the sanctuary. Someone played the piano, and the notes were reverent and haunting. Beautiful.

Sinclair.

Hope's eyes closed and her insides tightened

as she stood outside and listened. What went through his mind while he played? Did he ever think of her?

Opening her eyes, she pushed those kinds of wishes aside. Why would he think of her anyway? Just because she thought of him constantly didn't mean he'd return the favor. Taking a deep breath, Hope opened the door and went inside.

Sinclair looked up when he heard the door open. He expected their worship leaders, Diane and Bud, to arrive soon to practice and didn't want to be in their way. Instead, he saw Hope standing in the doorway, and his pulse took an erratic skip.

Sunshine poured in behind her, making her look ethereal, like something he might have dreamed. Like something that might slip away if he tried to touch.

She stepped closer, and he noticed a dainty dragonfly clip worn in her hair, pulling some of her bangs over to the side. It only reinforced the fairylike image.

"Are you ready for your first sermon?" Her smile was sweet and conciliatory.

Were his nerves easy to see? "As ready as I'll ever be, I guess."

"Your outline looked good. 'God Changes Everything' is a catchy title." She smoothed the front of her skirt.

"Thanks." He slid down the long piano bench and patted the wood. "Wanna sit down?"

Her eyes widened, and she hesitated. Maybe she was a little nervous, too. But then she perched on the end of the bench, and her slim fingers caressed the piano keys.

"Do you play?" he asked.

"Not very well."

"Play something."

She let out a shaky laugh and launched into the simple beginner's piece called "Chopsticks."

After listening to her for a few moments, he joined her on the lower end of the keys. For a solid five minutes they played together, filling the sanctuary with carefree music. The connection through the simple song made him forget the distance that had grown between them.

Watching Hope concentrate so hard on touching the right keys delighted him. She'd always taken every task seriously. When she caught her bottom lip between white teeth, he stared at her soft beauty. Why had he never before noticed how pretty she was, especially up close? He forgot that he'd placed her off-limits and hit the wrong note.

She laughed and turned toward him. "Where did you learn to play the piano? I don't remember you playing before."

"My mother wanted us kids to play Grandma Marsh's old piano in the living room, but I was the only one who kept at my lessons until high school. I took more lessons in college from a music major I was trying to impress."

Hope smiled again. "Did you?"

"Impress her?"

She nodded.

"No. She went after a football player. But I realized how easy it was to connect with God through music. Different maybe, but playing helps me focus."

"I should let you get back to it." Hope started to get up.

"Stay." He touched the soft skin of her arm. She calmed his nerves but rattled his senses.

She didn't move; she stared at his fingers still resting on her forearm.

He let his hand drop and cleared his throat. "This morning I'm going to announce a building committee meeting held after this Wednesday's service. We need to move forward on the project."

Her gaze flashed to his. "Have you decided what to build?"

"That'll be the main topic of discussion. We'll need to get a rough idea of how a youth center compares financially to the preschool. I'll need your input."

"What about opening it up to the congregation?"

"Once we have a decision from the board, we'll do that."

He knew how much Hope wanted that preschool, yet she'd look for acceptance from the whole church. She wasn't trying to ramrod her way like a certain board member with a nephew. He appreciated that. He appreciated too much about his office manager.

The worship team tromped into the sanctuary, their laughter loud and distracting. Sinclair cast them a glance and waved.

Hope got up to leave. "I better make sure Shannon has everything she needs for children's church."

"You'll be back for the service?" He wanted her opinion on his message. If he were truthful, he'd admit that he wanted her assurance. He didn't want to let his congregation down on his first Sunday service. He didn't want to let Hope down, either.

She nodded. "I'll be there."

After Walt and his wife, Carol, rang the church's bell, Hope took her seat in the fourth-row pew as always. She ignored the creeping disappointment that her parents really weren't coming. She'd hoped they'd finally show.

It proved difficult to concentrate during the short worship service. She'd close her eyes, only to open them and find herself staring at the back of Sinclair's head. He wore a nice suit for his first Sunday message, but no tie. He preferred T-shirts underneath his button-downs. After working with him for a week, Sinclair seemed different—but had he really changed?

She'd done her best to keep her distance. Wednesday night, she should have remained downstairs with the children's program instead of making arrangements to hear Sinclair's first message. Ever since she'd heard him talk about Haiti, she'd felt drawn to him in a way that irritated her. She wasn't ready to forgive him. She shouldn't want anything to do with him, but after all these years, Sinclair still fascinated her. Now maybe even more.

When greeting time rolled around after the kids had been dismissed for children's church, Hope hit the aisles. She chatted with people she'd known most of her life. She bounced off questions about her parents' whereabouts with vague answers. But some of them looked like they'd guessed the reason, even if they didn't say a word. They remembered Sara's accident. They remembered that both Sinclair and Ryan Marsh had been there that day.

"Good morning, Hope."

Hope halted her steps when she recognized Bob and Rose Marsh. Of course they'd attend their son's church. She hadn't thought about it, nor had she prepared for it. Especially when Sinclair had told her that Eva and her fiancé were counseling at their own church—the church both of their families had attended when they were teens.

Pressing on her stomach to quell the rush of memories, Hope drew in a deep breath and then reached out her hands. "Mr. and Mrs. Marsh, nice to see you."

Sinclair's diminutive mom enveloped her in a warm hug instead. "You look wonderful, Hope. How are you?"

Hope didn't meet Rose's direct gaze. The woman could see right through a person, and Hope didn't want to be read like an open book. "Good, thanks. And you both?"

"Retirement agrees with us, right, Bob?" Rose elbowed her husband.

"Sure does."

"But you're here for the summer, right?" Hope remembered how Rose used to invite her to stay for dinner, along with Sara. Sara had often raved about how the Marsh family had been tight. Were they still?

"Yep, helping Eva and Adam with the orchard. By the way, we're having a party—"

"Hey, Mom," Sinclair interrupted with a hand on Rose's shoulder. "We're about to get started."

"So these are your parents?" Mary Stillwell moved in. "You must be so proud. Sinclair, you have to introduce them to the church body."

"Ah, yeah. Mom, Dad, this is Mary Stillwell."

"My husband, Chuck, is on the board."

"We've met before. Stillwell is one of the largest commercial growers in the county," Bob Marsh said. "How'd he fare the storm a couple weeks back?"

Mary gave an awkward laugh like she didn't dare give any information away to a competing grower. "Time will tell, right?"

Hope noticed that Sinclair looked flustered when Chuck joined the circle and started talking cherries with his dad. Marsh Orchards had never been close in scale to Stillwell Farms, but Bob Marsh still wore his pride openly. He bragged about the big plans his future son-in-law had for their orchard.

"I better get us back on track," Sinclair whispered close to Hope's ear, and briefly caressed her arm.

His touch made her shiver. She caught Rose Marsh's eye, and Hope's heart sank when she saw the woman's smile grow a little wider.

Sinclair's voice came over the microphone, calling the parishioners back to their seats. "It's nice to know I'm in a church where greeting time turns into full-blown fellowship. I can't wait to see what the potlucks are like."

Hope sat down amid the good-natured murmurs and laughs. The church hadn't had a potluck in months, so hearing Sinclair mention looking forward to one might as well have been an invitation to schedule one. No doubt Mrs. Larson was already thumbing through her calendar to pick a date. And Hope would get a call from her tomorrow, prodding her to make plans.

Hope's fingers gripped the edge of her pew as Sinclair took the podium. Why did it matter so much how well he did this morning? He looked natural and composed, except for the tightness of his jaw as he introduced his parents. And then he joked about keeping *this* message clean, and Hope felt her tension ease.

Then Sinclair prayed, and she noticed something different about him. His stance seemed firmer and his shoulders a little broader as he opened up his Bible and straightened his notes. There was a gleam in his eye as Sinclair boldly read a passage from chapter three in Philippians. He didn't read with the carefree charm she'd expected. Sinclair spoke with confidence about forgetting the past and looking forward to the future by trusting God.

His deep voice rang out with conviction. Hearing him speak with such fire made her skin prickle into goose bumps. And yet there was humbleness in him, too, like the day he'd approached her parents. She'd seen a peek of that then.

He talked about how God had changed him. He admitted that he'd made mistakes and didn't have all the answers. He advised everyone to put their trust in God, because Sinclair would most likely let them down.

When he looked directly at her, Hope had to swallow the lump of emotion that rose in her throat. His eyes blazed with contrition, and Hope couldn't look away.

When Sinclair moved on to reference the next scripture verse, Hope looked around the sanctuary. The congregation was transfixed, held captive by words spoken with truth. Words that closed with an invitation to those who wanted to put their trust in the Lord to come forward.

A couple of people answered the altar call, and Hope felt a wash of pride for her new pastor. If anyone could rally this church body around a building project, it was Sinclair. She could see that now. If only she could be sure which project he'd get behind.

After the service concluded, several people rushed to the platform in order to shake Sinclair's hand. That was as good a sign as any that their new pastor had been officially accepted.

Hope made for the exit with her insides twisted into a ball of old and new feelings. She was proud of Sinclair, but something else swirled inside her heart that was too dangerous to name and too scary to let loose.

Walking outside into the warm sunshine, she sorted out those disturbing emotions concerning her boss, pastor and longtime friend. He'd let her down so many times. But then she'd had unrealistic expectations of him. Dreams.

Hope boxed up those dreams and put them away like she'd done a hundred times before. Tamping her feelings down deep, she refused to care for Sinclair all over again.

Not looking where she was going, Hope bumped right into Rose Marsh. "Oh, sorry, excuse me."

Rose smiled and then pushed a small envelope into her hand. "Please come."

It looked like an invitation. Hope tipped her head.

"Eva and Adam's engagement party. Eva would love to see you."

"Oh, I don't know..." Hope searched for an excuse but came up short. She couldn't find the words to refuse. Wasn't sure she wanted to.

"Don't worry about Sinclair. Don't worry about calling to RSVP. Just come." Rose patted her hand and left.

Hope stood in the parking lot, staring at the envelope. If Sinclair had truly changed, seeing him with his family would prove it.

After tearing open the seal, Hope read the date and sucked in a breath.

Saturday night at Marsh Orchards.

This Saturday would have been Sara's twenty-fifth birthday. They couldn't have known when they had scheduled the party. Ryan might not have even remembered. If he had, she couldn't imagine him saying anything about it to dampen his sister's joy.

Hope had run into Ryan a few times in town, and every time she'd seen him, he'd looked lost. She supposed they all were, to an extent.

How could she go and not break her parents' hearts? Yet watching them try not to fall apart wasn't something she wanted to do. She couldn't face another year staying home to grieve. Her sister would never want that kind of morose tribute.

Hope looked back and spotted Sinclair talking to several people on the steps outside the sanctuary. He met her gaze and cocked his head, almost as if he could see the struggle inside her.

She gave him a quick wave and headed for her car. In the driver's seat, she fingered the invitation with its pretty pink parchment paper and fancy lettering promising a happy occasion. She wanted to accept that promise, but at what price?

Stuffing the invitation back in the envelope, Hope started her car and headed out of the parking lot with a whispered prayer for direction. She knew from experience that following your heart wasn't always the best decision.

She shouldn't go. Plain and simple.

But she had six days to decide what to do. Plenty of time to change her mind.

Chapter Four

Sinclair stopped by his office at church to pick up a business card he'd left there over the weekend. He also wanted to hear Hope's thoughts on Sunday's message. She'd give him an honest answer.

Hope's opinion had always been important to him, but now it seemed vital. She knew the church so well. She knew the people and their expectations. She'd tell him if he'd missed the mark. Although he didn't think he had.

"What are you doing here? Monday is your day off." Hope caught him in the hallway between offices.

He lifted the business card. "I'm meeting a distributor of prefabricated commercial buildings to get some quotes. Wanna go with me?"

Hope glanced back at her desk.

"Shannon can cover the phones. Come on, it'll

only take a couple hours. I could use your help in asking the right questions."

When she didn't look convinced, Sinclair added what he hoped was additional incentive. "I'll buy lunch."

Hope's eyes narrowed. "I don't know...."

Her hesitation bit him. There used to be a time when she'd had no reservations toward him. When it was a piece of cake to get her to play hooky. Only this wasn't playing hooky. It was building project work, and it was important.

"Come on," he whispered and then waited.

She finally gave in. "Okay, I'll get my purse."

He smiled and followed her into the main office.

Shannon looked up. "Where are you guys off to?"

"Traverse City. We're looking at construction options for Wednesday's building committee meeting." Sinclair leaned against Hope's desk.

Shannon's grin widened. "Now that sounds like too much fun to handle."

No matter how hard he tried to hide his attraction to Hope, when it came to the receptionist, Sinclair got the feeling that Shannon saw right through him. "Gotta start comparing costs somewhere."

She gave him an encouraging nod.

"You've got my cell if anything comes up." Hope slung her purse over her shoulder.

"Don't worry, I can man the fort."

"Thanks, Shannon." Sinclair shook his head at the wink she gave him before following Hope out the door.

This outing might be work related, but Sinclair looked forward to spending time alone with Hope. He wanted to know more about her plans for the preschool. He wanted to know more about her and the woman she'd become while he'd been gone.

When they reached his car, he opened the passenger side door for her—something he'd never done before.

Hope looked surprised. "Thanks."

"You're welcome." He waited for her to buckle in before shutting the door.

Slipping behind the wheel, Sinclair was all too aware of her sitting next to him. He'd missed her. Missed their friendship. After all that had happened, could they go back?

"How far?"

Sinclair glanced at her as he turned down the air-conditioning. "What's that?"

"How far is this place?" Hope wore pink pants with a matching top that made her look ultrafeminine. Pretty. She sat up straight with her hands folded in her lap, staring at the road ahead.

He could see the tension in her shoulders. She wasn't comfortable around him. "Just west of Traverse City. Not far."

"How'd you find out about it?"

"My dad gave me the guy's card. I called and set up an appointment." Sinclair had gone to the office Saturday evening to prepare for Sunday's sermon and had made the plans then.

Hope stared at her hands. "Your mom gave me an invitation to your sister's party."

He kept his focus on the road. "Are you going?"

"I don't know if I should."

"Eva would love to see you." Sinclair wasn't so sure about Ryan.

"What about you?" She looked at him then, but her expression was hard to read. She looked calm and composed, like always.

Talk about a no-brainer. He'd love to see her there, too. Would love to dance with her, hold her. But that wasn't wise, considering the situation with her parents. "What about your folks?"

Hope shrugged. "They might not understand."

"Whatever you decide, my mom will be fine. And so will I." There. He hadn't encouraged her one way or the other. That was safe enough.

"Thanks." Hope smiled, and her features relaxed. A little.

"You're welcome." Sinclair noticed the way she curled her hair behind one ear. The edge of her dusky waves swirled at the sweet spot of her neck, right along the line of her jaw.

She glanced at him, her cheeks a little rosier than a minute ago. "What?"

"Nothing. Nothing at all." He turned his attention back where it belonged before they ended up in a ditch.

When they pulled into the parking lot, Hope spotted a couple of pole buildings erected in a field and knew this wasn't the right option. Their church was old and quaint, with white clapboard siding and a bell tower. A pole building stuck to the side would never fly. It'd be ugly.

She didn't wait for Sinclair to open her door, even though he was headed around the front of the car by the time Hope got out.

"Just keep an open mind, okay?" he said.

"I haven't said a word."

"No, but you're scowling."

"These are glorified pole barns."

"I know." Sinclair flashed her that boyish smile. "Let's see what the guy has to say."

The guy headed straight for them with a clipboard and dripping eagerness to make a sale. He held out his hand. "Afternoon, folks. You're Bob Marsh's son, right?"

"I am." He pumped the guy's hand. "I'm Sinclair Marsh, and this is my office manager, Hope Petersen. We're looking at options for our church."

The guy scanned his clipboard. "A small gym, right?"

"Or classrooms," Hope added.

The salesman gave her an indifferent nod and focused his attention back on Sinclair. Talking the whole way to the showroom about low maintenance and ease of construction, he didn't take a breath.

Hope wasn't sold. There was no way they'd meet state requirements for an early education classroom. She pulled out a pad of paper from her purse and jotted down some questions. Could the exterior be altered to match an existing building? What about future expansion?

In the showroom, portions of completed structures were displayed to give the buyer an idea of available options. Some looked like building trailers and makeshift office space, but nothing looked comparable to classrooms. The windows were small and few. Kids needed windows to let in lots of light.

After a brief video presentation, the salesman looked ready to talk nuts and bolts. "You mentioned a youth center and classrooms—here's how we can achieve multipurpose usage."

Hope leaned forward as the salesman sketched out a stand-alone building, again with few windows. The inside would have a gymnasium floor, basketball hoops and a small stage area.

"We've created these for other churches, and there are plenty of electrical hookups for music. The stage serves as a platform for youth ministry as well as theatrical events."

"How would you accommodate classrooms?" Hope said, before Sinclair could speak.

"We can order dividers that convert the space into rooms."

Hope didn't like the sound of that.

"What kind of estimates are we looking at? As well as time to construct?" Sinclair gave her a pointed look to jot down the answer.

"Let me show you some examples, along with the associated costs."

Hope tried not to fidget as they took virtual tours into several multipurpose pole buildings. Some were indeed impressive. And expensive. The better options came with higher price tags and bigger units.

After Sinclair requested information on a couple of different, less expensive models, the salesman created a spiffy brochure to hand out at the building committee meeting.

"Can you alter the exterior to match an existing structure?" Hope asked.

The salesman cocked his head. "What kind of structure?"

"An addition to a clapboard-sided church, for instance?"

"All our buildings are metal sided for durability."

After a few more virtual tours, more quotes and brochures, Sinclair led Hope toward his car. "You don't like any of them, do you?"

"Don't you think parents would prefer their kids in the same building during services?"

He shrugged, clearly not following her logic. "I guess."

"Teenagers heading off to a separate place might be one thing, but little ones? Think of the security issues. How do we monitor who's coming and going from a separate location?"

"All things to consider."

Hope shook her head. "I'll check into zoning requirements for prefabricated buildings before the meeting."

"Sounds good." He grinned, obviously relieved to leave the details to her. "Now, what would you like for lunch?"

"Doesn't matter to me."

"I know the perfect place then."

Fifteen minutes later, they were seated at a small café table in a swank Traverse City restaurant. Glancing around at the French provincial decor, she lowered the fancy menu, complete with an extensive wine list. "Are you sure about this?"

"Eva says the sandwiches are awesome."

Looking more closely at the menu, Hope realized that the lunch prices were almost reasonable. At least they were outside, on a patio that overlooked the main street filled with shoppers and traffic. It was far from an intimate setting, and if their conversation lagged they could people watch.

Once they gave their orders, Sinclair leaned on his elbows toward her. "What did you think of yesterday's message? No complaint calls?"

By the worried look on his face, she didn't think he was fishing for compliments. "No complaints. Actually, it was good. Really good."

"Good." He gave her a satisfied smile. Sinclair had always been so cocky and confident—he'd never needed assurance like this before. She liked this change. It made him seem more humble. And attractive.

"I'll work in more of the needs in Haiti a little later. If we can find room in the missions budget, I'd like to support the school there. Maybe even plan a couple trips. The experience changes lives."

"Whose lives are impacted? The people in Haiti or those who visit?" Hope believed in missions, but was the cost to send a bunch of people with no plans to become missionaries worth the expense? "Seems to me that sending money instead of people would meet more needs."

"Depends on the need and who's the needy one." Sinclair looked serious, something she wasn't quite used to. "Making money stretch is what God does. Multiplying the loaves of bread and fishes wasn't just for biblical times. God can make a difference in a willing heart, and that's worth way more than cash."

"Haiti changed you, didn't it?"

He nodded. "Starting with my name."

Hope cocked her head. "Your name?"

"It didn't feel right being called Sin, and it was too confusing with translation. Besides, I didn't *want* it to fit anymore. Who'd go to a church with a pastor called Sin?"

Hope laughed. "You'd be surprised."

"I suppose you're right, but using my full name makes my mom happy. She never liked the nickname."

Hope streaked her finger down the water glass in front of her before glancing at Sinclair. "Me neither."

He gave her another toe-curling smile. "All the better, then."

Hope quickly sipped water to calm the flutters in her belly. Sinclair Marsh was not flirting with her, was he? The waitress delivered their order, saving her from having to respond or reflect any further.

After Sinclair offered up a brief prayer of thanks, they dug into their sandwiches. His sister had been right about the food. Hope stifled a groan of pleasure after her first bite of a turkey club slathered with avocado.

"Tell me why a preschool should be built."

Hope swallowed but didn't answer right away.

"Other than offering Christian education, I think it's important to support the single moms in our community."

"How?"

Hope shifted. She wasn't used to Sinclair listening so intently, as if he'd tuned everything out around them to focus on her. "There's a woman at church who lost her job due to layoffs. She took a lower-paying one and can no longer afford to send her girls to day care during the summer. Her girls are at their grandmother's for a couple weeks, but when they get home, they're on their own while Mom's at work. The oldest is nine."

His eyes narrowed. "So how does tuition-based preschool solve that?"

"The tuition could help offset expenses for a summer day program." Hope tamped down the excitement bubbling inside.

Sinclair looked thoughtful and interested, like a lightbulb had just gone off inside his head. "You've figured this out?"

"Yup. I mean, I have estimates."

"Let's look at those before the committee meeting." Sinclair polished off the rest of his sandwich.

Hope nodded and took another bite of her turkey club, glad that she'd caved in when Sinclair had asked her to go with him today. It was easier to talk shop here rather than in the office with phone interruptions and folks constantly coming and going for appointments with Sinclair.

Silence stretched while she finished her food, and Sinclair signaled their waitress for the check. And then Hope felt him looking at her. "Why do you keep looking at me? Do I have mayo on my chin?"

He laughed. "No. I was wondering when you got rid of your glasses."

Hope shrugged. "A couple of years ago. It's too hard to run with glasses—they slip off my nose."

Surprise spread across his face. "You run?"

A prickly feeling scurried up her back. She'd rather discuss church or the preschool. He looked at her with a kernel of admiration that she found more disarming than any taste of wine from the fancy menu. "I started in college but wasn't consistent until a couple years ago."

Running quieted her mind. Dismissed the sorrow-filled thoughts of Sara and the what-ifs that plagued her. "What about you? You used to wear contacts."

"Not practical in Haiti. I'm used to wearing the spectacles now." He wiggled his eyebrows at her. "Makes me look older, don't you think?"

"I don't know about that." No way was she going to tell him that his haunted eyes with lines etched at the corners made him look older. He was thinner, too. His clothes sort of hung off him.

He switched gears on her by turning curious. Those haunted hazel eyes searched hers. "You never made it to Spain, did you?"

"No." She wiped her mouth with her napkin and draped it over her plate.

"Why not? You were stoked for that trip."

"I couldn't leave my parents to grieve alone."

Sinclair's expression of disappointment and regret tugged at her heart. His voice softened. "I'm sorry."

Hope shrugged because she didn't trust herself to speak. She couldn't tell him it was okay when it wasn't. Too many things had changed the day he dared her sister to do something stupid.

The waitress came with the check and Sinclair took care of it.

She gave him a smile. "Thank you."

"Lunch was good." He smiled back, then rose to pull out her chair.

Hope turned toward him. "So was the conversation."

"And your company." Despite the grin on Sinclair's face, his eyes looked thoughtful. Serious. He wasn't teasing her. He wasn't flirting, either. He meant what he said.

Hope stepped away from him. Lunch was over. They needed to get back to work and the safety of the office.

By the time they made it back, Hope was sleepy,

full and more confused about Sinclair than ever. Settling into her office chair, she looked up to find Shannon standing near her desk with a handful of pink message slips.

"How'd it go?"

"Fine. We gathered a lot of information. Which reminds me, I need to check with zoning because I don't believe we can attach anything prefabricated to the church. It's got to mesh with the existing dwelling."

Shannon rolled her eyes. "That's not what I meant."

"Shan—" Hope stopped when she spotted Sinclair coming toward them.

"Do either of you need anything before I take off?"

"Nope, we're good," Hope answered.

His gaze lingered. "Thanks for going with me today. And thank you, Shannon, for covering the office. I'll see you both tomorrow."

After he'd left, Shannon turned on her with wide eyes and a grin. "So? Tell me what happened."

"Nothing *happened*." Not quite true. Hope had melted a little more toward Sinclair. "We saw the prefab guy, went to lunch and then we came back. End of story."

"Uh-huh." Shannon wasn't buying it.

Hope gave her friend a mock glare. "Now leave me alone. I have work to do."

"Where'd he take you?"

Hope sighed. "To that French restaurant downtown."

"Oooh. Nice. So our young pastor has good taste, I see." Shannon looked smug.

"I guess." Hope shrugged. "His sister recommends the sandwiches. And she's right. They're awesome."

She'd be stupid to think Sinclair took her there for any other reason than because Eva said it was a good place. He wasn't trying to impress her. Wishing for more than a friendly work relationship invited a barrelful of hurt she was in no mood to experience all over again. But tell that to the butterflies dancing inside her stomach whenever Sinclair looked at her. And today, he'd looked far too often.

"Well, I'm leaving, too." Shannon quickly tidied her desk. "By the way, your mom called."

Guilt washed through Hope like she'd had her hand in the proverbial cookie jar. "What did you tell her?"

Shannon shrugged. "That you went to Traverse City with the pastor."

Hope's insides rolled. *Great.*

"Was I not supposed to say so?" Shannon looked stricken.

"No, no. It's fine." But Hope knew she'd have some explaining to do when she got home.

"Is everything okay between your parents and Sinclair?"

It wasn't okay, and it might never be okay. "He was helping cut hay the day my sister got killed. Bad memories there."

Although she trusted Shannon, Hope didn't want to chance rumors about Sinclair's involvement in the accident. Not with him as their new pastor. Not many people knew the details of Sara's death, and Hope preferred that it stayed that way.

"Wow. I'm so sorry. No wonder they didn't attend service yesterday. He must be a reminder of what happened."

"Yeah." Hope had never told Shannon the whole story. She and her husband moved to the area shortly after the accident, and they'd helped Hope through some dark times.

"Is that what's keeping you from letting Sinclair know you're interested?"

"Who says I'm interested?" Hope didn't mean to answer so sharply.

Shannon laughed. "You do. Every time you try *not* to look at him."

Hope was grateful the phone rang. She gave Shannon a cheery wave because the caller ID promised a lengthy call. Mrs. Larson wasn't ever brief. Still, her friend's words pestered her.

Hope couldn't allow her working relationship with Sinclair to become infected by their past. But feelings long since buried, yet never forgotten, pricked her like an annoying sliver.

Slivers needed to be pulled out before they became inflamed and too sore to touch.

Chapter Five

The building committee meeting held after Wednesday night's service came quickly, and Sinclair wasn't looking forward to it. Hope had updated quotes for the addition from a couple local builders they'd used the first time around, and it was no surprise they were more costly than the prefab.

What had surprised him was the state requirement for room sizes of a new preschool center. Those requirements would force the committee, and then ultimately the board, to choose—youth center or preschool. There was no mixing the two when it came to their budget.

"You look worried." Judy Graves refilled her water bottle from the church's kitchen sink.

"We've got some hard choices ahead of us."

"Doing the right thing isn't usually the easy route."

Sinclair knew that truth on several levels. "Tell me about it."

Judy smiled and patted his shoulder. "You'll figure it out."

She had more confidence in him than he did. Get behind the youth center, and Sinclair crushed Hope's dream. Push for the preschool, and he risked the possibility of losing the church's largest financial contributor.

Could he stay neutral and pray the board came to their own decision? He wasn't one to take the coward's way out, but he wasn't ready to make his decision. Not yet.

He slipped into a chair as Hope called the meeting to order. She passed out the information they'd gathered the past couple of days, and then looked at him to take over.

Might as well get this thing started. Pushing his glasses up the bridge of his nose, Sinclair stood. "What Hope gave you are estimates for a preschool addition and a small prefabricated building for a youth center—"

"Why can't we do both in the prefab?" Chuck Stillwell interrupted.

"The state doesn't allow for a new preschool that small. Licensing standards require certain dimensions for classroom sizes, so that knocks out the multipurpose plan."

"But the addition isn't that much larger," one of the elders, who was also a board member, added.

"We can use our existing basement to meet

some of those requirements, namely the kitchen and quiet time space. There's some leeway with an addition to an existing structure, namely a church," Sinclair explained.

"And a preschool will charge tuition that can help offset some initial costs," Hope offered.

"But there arc overhead costs, such as staff, to consider. We wouldn't have those, other than a youth pastor, with a youth center," Chuck pointed out.

And that's when the debate picked up steam and charged out of control. Chuck championed the youth center. He campaigned that it'd be a good place to also foster a men's fellowship group because of indoor basketball. Judy stood firm for the preschool, arguing that early education was more important than men and their sports.

After the arguments blew their course, the group looked to their pastor for his opinion. Sinclair couldn't give it. Not when he agreed with both sides of the issue. He wanted to make Hope happy, but that was not a good enough motive to vote for the preschool. He didn't want to be swayed by Chuck, either.

"I suggest we table a decision until next week's meeting. In the interim, I think we should list the pros and cons for each and tackle the subject from a more analytical perspective." Sinclair glanced at Hope, knowing she'd been waiting a long time for this.

She didn't look pleased, and he couldn't blame her. He'd made her wait yet again.

By the end of the week, Hope was strung out. Sinclair had run her ragged following up on estimates for a larger prefabricated building and zoning restrictions. A flurry of lunch dates and appointments with parishioners kept Sinclair busy, too, as well as taking over for Walt, their maintenance guy who'd called out for the rest of the week with a sprained ankle.

She had to hand it to Sinclair. He was settling in like a real pastor, mowing the lawn and helping clean the restrooms without complaint. The only nit she could pick was that he didn't have a vision. Not for the building project or the church, other than what he'd told her that day at lunch about missions support for the school in Haiti. That wasn't enough to inspire a congregation.

The sound of tromping feet caught her attention as two blonde little girls raced into the office. They sidled up to her desk.

"Hi, Miss Hope." Nine-year-old Hannah slipped into a chair.

"How was your visit with your grandmother?" Hope asked.

"Boring." Grace, the recently turned seven-year-old missing her front teeth, slouched against the wall.

Hope chuckled. "Why boring?"

"Grandma wouldn't take us swimming. All she had was a silly little pool."

Hope imagined that a plastic kiddie pool was no match for Lake Leelanau, where the girls were used to going with their mom. "Ah, I see. What are you up to now? Does your mom know you're over here?"

"I called her." Hannah stood a little taller. As the big sister in charge, she took her role seriously. "After work, we're going to the building site for our house. Mom says we can help."

"That'll be fun," Hope said.

Dorrie had applied for and received a grant toward a newly built home for low-income families. It had been a long process, and they'd finally broken ground this spring. Dorrie said she had a better appreciation for what Hope was up against with the red tape of a preschool.

"Sometimes we have pizza there." Grace loved pizza.

"That makes it extra special then. Would you girls like to help me fold and stuff bulletins while you're here? I can't offer pizza, but we have some milk and homemade cookies in the fridge."

"Sure." The tandem response from the girls

didn't lack enthusiasm. They'd had Shannon's homemade chocolate chip cookies before.

Hope fetched the box of bulletin copies and Sinclair's outlined message insert. She stationed the girls at Shannon's desk since she'd left for the day and put them to work folding and stuffing. "Like this, see?"

The girls nodded and grabbed for the goods.

Hope watched them fold and stuff the first few copies, making sure they knew what they were doing.

"When did we get new employees?" Sinclair stood near Hope's desk with his hands on hips, an exaggerated stern look on his face. "I didn't approve any new hires."

Both girls giggled.

Hope smiled. "Pastor Sinclair, these are Dorrie Cavanaugh's girls." She touched each one's head. "This is Hannah, and this is Grace. They're here to volunteer."

"Oh, well, that's different. Volunteers are special." Sinclair bowed with a flourish, making the girls giggle again. "Pleased to meet you both. Is Miss Hope working you too hard?"

"She gives us fun jobs." Grace spoke in a lisp through her missing teeth.

"And cookies," Hannah added.

Sinclair gave Hope a smile. "She's a smart lady."

Hannah nodded. "Yup. Mom says Miss Hope is the best kept secret in northern Michigan."

"Your mom is right about that." Sinclair gave Hope a smile that zapped those butterflies back to life with a vengeance. "And I better let you two get to work."

Hope followed Sinclair to the kitchen so she could fetch the promised snack. "You don't mind if they're here, do you?"

"No. Not at all, as long as they don't bother you."

Did that mean interfere with her work? "They live in that old mobile home across the hayfield. I've got all kinds of odd jobs to keep them busy when they stop in."

Sinclair studied her. "It's not your responsibility to watch them."

Hope had told him about these girls the other day at lunch, and he still didn't get it. He didn't see their need.

"I feel better knowing they're all right. This is their first summer home alone. Their mom calls them often to check in, but I want them to know it's okay to come here if they need anything."

He smiled at her. A sweet, soft kind of smile. "You take care of everyone, don't you?"

She squared her shoulders, not sure if he was complimenting her or if he meant that she was a pathetic sucker. "Aren't we supposed to take care of each other? The church body and all that?"

"Yeah, we are."

She was caught by the tender look in his eyes. She couldn't make her feet move, even though her brain warned her to turn tail and run. There were so many snares for her when it came to Sinclair.

"Miss Hope? We ran out of inserts." Hannah stood in the doorway.

"No problem. I've got more. Come on, I'll show you where." Hope herded the girl back to the office without a backward glance.

By the end of the day, Hope hadn't decided how to tell her parents that she planned to go to Eva Marsh's engagement party. She was an adult, but she might as well be back in high school, waiting for that right moment to ask for permission to go to a party after a football game.

Driving home, she mentally ran through her list of logical reasons not to tell them anything. She was twenty-seven and had the right to some privacy. They were going downstate to a farm equipment auction anyway. She should simply tell her folks that she was going out and leave it at that in case they called. She didn't like to make anyone worry.

Still in her work clothes, Hope plopped on the living room couch and grabbed the TV remote.

Turning to the local news, she figured she'd let tomorrow night's weather forecast confirm her decision. If it was going to rain, she might stay home.

Her mother came into the room with a small suitcase in hand. "Your dad and I are heading out. I left the number of the hotel by the phone if you need anything."

Now was her chance to say something, but Hope only nodded. "I'll be fine. When will you be back?"

"Sunday." Her mother's chin lifted slightly.

"Good for you." Hope was glad her folks weren't going to spend another year grieving at home. And they wouldn't be around Saturday night.

"You'll be okay here alone?" her mom asked.

Hope spotted her father in the doorway, looking concerned and almost as guilty as her mom for going away. "Of course I'll be okay. Tomorrow night, I'm going to an engagement party."

When her mother's brow furrowed, Hope bounced up and gave her mom a hug before she could ask any questions. "Go and have a nice weekend away. You both deserve it."

"Don't forget to feed the horses. I dropped hay for the beef cattle that should last all weekend."

Hope gave her dad a hug, too. "I'll take care of it."

Her parents looked hesitant, but Hope shooed them with her hands. "Go. Go. I'll be fine."

After exchanged looks of relief, her parents left, leaving behind a quiet house.

Hope slumped back onto the couch and the dog jumped up next to her. She scratched behind Gypsy's ear. "Looks like it's you and me this weekend."

The dog's tongue lolled out the side of her mouth, and then she butted her head under Hope's hand, wanting more love.

Hope laughed and gave in.

With her folks out of town, did she really need to explain why she wanted to go to Eva Marsh's engagement party? Hope didn't fully understand herself. It had been hard enough answering her mother's questions about why she'd gone to Traverse City with Sinclair. Her mom didn't believe their meeting was work related or that lunch had been simply lunch. Her mother hadn't complained about it though, nor had she looked a bit surprised.

If her father knew about it, he hadn't said anything.

All Hope knew was that spending what would have been Sara's twenty-fifth birthday at home was not an option for any of them. Not this year.

Saturday night, Hope parked her car on the road in front of the Marsh Orchards sign. It allowed for an early getaway. An easy one if needed. She breathed in the warm evening air. The grass had been cut earlier and its sweet earthy scent still smelled strong and fresh.

It was the perfect kind of summer night with a balmy feel to the soft breeze that stirred her senses. This was the kind of night for romance, and longing spread through Hope. She wanted dates and flowers and candy.... If only the risk of heartache didn't go along with all that.

She spotted the big ball of orange sun hanging low in the hazy western sky and forced herself to think practical thoughts. It'd be a couple hours before dark. She'd stay only until then.

Hope's insides clenched as she walked up the Marsh family's long driveway lined with cars. Spotting the cheerful farmhouse painted the color of ripe sweet cherries pinched her heart. It had been years since the last time she'd been here, and memories of Sara swirled through her mind.

They'd played on the old wooden swing hanging from a huge maple tree in the front yard. She could even hear Sara's squeals as she chased Ryan with water balloons during a Fourth of July picnic. Once upon a time, their families had been friends and attended the same church with a large youth group. She'd met Sinclair in that youth group.

Memories of him crashed into her thoughts and took over. As a kid, she used to hang out with him on the porch to watch the sun go down or play catch in the yard. Sometimes, she had helped finish his chores so they could go for bike rides. The images were a flash flood of painful reminders of her shame. She used to follow him around like a puppy.

Was she doing that again?

Working with Sinclair was interesting and new, and she'd kept their bittersweet past, for the most part, in the past. But tonight was different. Time had somehow wound its way backward, and she couldn't stop the images swirling in her mind or the feelings they conjured up.

Maybe this wasn't such a good idea. Smoothing the front of the filmy summer dress she'd purchased in Toronto, Hope gathered her courage. She could leave now and no one would know.

Too late. Rose Marsh intercepted her. "Hope, I'm so glad you came. And you look lovely."

She managed a wobbly, "Thank you. Thank you for the invite."

Rose stepped closer and touched her elbow. "You okay?"

"There are so many memories here." Hope blinked back sudden tears.

"I know." Rose gave her arm a comforting squeeze. "Hard to face sometimes, but we need to do it anyway."

Hope nodded.

Rose had suffered, too, if those new lines etched around her eyes and mouth were any indication.

She'd lost a future daughter-in-law, and Sinclair had taken off for Haiti with no clue when he'd return. And they'd sold their orchard.

Hope pulled herself together. "Where do I go?"

Rose smiled and then pointed. "At the start of the orchard, we've set up a big tent. Bathrooms are in the house and pole barn. You go on ahead. I have to grab more iced tea from the fridge."

"Need help?"

"Nope, you go." Rose smiled even wider, reminding her of Sinclair.

Everything here reminded her of Sinclair— the boy and young man he used to be. But he'd changed. He was different at work. Would he be different here?

Hope made her way toward the large white canopy tent that was positioned at the highest part of the sloping orchard with views of both lakes— Lake Leelanau and Lake Michigan just beyond. Tent poles were wound with white netting and white lights and clusters of wild daisies. Even though it'd be a while before the sky grew dark, the mood was already festive.

The sound of people's chatter mixed with the band warming up calmed her somewhat, but she felt far from relaxed. Stepping under the tent, she glanced around. Light hors d'oeuvres probably made by Sinclair's aunt lay spread on a long table. Glass canisters of chilled lemonade and iced tea were melting in the heat. Glass bottles of soft drinks and other beverages were placed in metal tubs filled with ice.

She spotted Sinclair surrounded by several women, some she recognized from high school. Again, that pinch to her heart made her question her presence. He wasn't wearing his glasses tonight, and when he laughed, he looked like his carefree old self. Even more handsome, though.

"Hope!" Eva Marsh waved.

Sinclair's sister nearly knocked her down with a hearty hug. "Wow, look at you. How are you?"

Hope smiled. "I'm good. And you look so happy. You're radiant."

"I am happy. Deliriously so." Eva grabbed her hand. "Come with me. You have to meet Adam."

They wove their way through a throng of people, and Hope recognized Ryan Marsh before he saw her. He chuckled at something a shorter man had said. That man looked like he might have walked off the pages of a men's fashion magazine. He was that strikingly handsome.

When they stopped in front of him, Hope swallowed her surprise.

"This is Adam Peece, my fiancé. Adam, this is Hope Petersen."

Hope shook Adam's hand. He had the brightest blue eyes she'd ever seen. "Nice to meet you, and congratulations."

"Thanks. How do you know Eva?"

Hope glanced at Ryan. His brow furrowed, and the stark pain she read in his eyes made Hope want to run away. Fast. "We grew up together."

"All of us did." Eva looked at her brother with concern, like she'd momentarily forgotten and was sorry for dragging Hope along.

Hope wished she could disappear. But she'd come tonight hoping for closure, and that meant some discomfort along the way. She looked at Ryan and smiled.

"How's it going, Hope?" Ryan asked.

"Pretty good, and you?"

"I have my days."

"I know." There wasn't much else she could say. Today had to be one of those days, maybe the worst kind of day. Ryan had to be thinking about Sara turning twenty-five. A sensitive guy like him wouldn't forget, would he? Sara would have loved a party like this—outside at the end of a hot summer's day. That was her sister in a nutshell, sunny and warm.

And yet Ryan was here for Eva's sake.

"Excuse me." Ryan gave Adam a nod and stepped away.

Eva's fiancé looked a little confused until understanding dawned. "Hope Petersen...you're—"

"Sara was my sister," Hope said.

"I'm so sorry," Eva quickly added. "It's still hard for him."

"Really, it's fine." But it wasn't. It hurt. And Hope's heart broke for Ryan. Obviously, he hadn't moved on. But then, maybe she hadn't, either. Not really.

"I think it's good for him to see you," Adam said. "He tries too hard to forget her."

Hope nodded, her throat tight.

Eva squeezed her hand. "He's pretty close with my brother, so you can trust him on that one."

"There are memories all over this place." Hope's voice came out raw.

Adam wrapped his arm around Eva, pulling her close. "And we're ready to make new ones, right?"

"You know it." Eva looked at Hope. "Now, tell me what you've been up to."

Hope shrugged off her gloom and forced a smile. "Working at the church is pretty much it."

"Sinclair said that you do a great job." Eva grinned. "He'd be lost without you."

Warmth spread through Hope. He really did need her. But before she could dig for more information, another couple joined them. They fawned over Eva's half-carat engagement ring. Hope *oohed* and *aahed* along with them. She noticed how Adam's chest had puffed up with pride and how his eyes softened every time he looked at Eva.

Another twinge to Hope's heart. She wanted that. Eva was blessed to have found someone who fulfilled her dreams, and it was obvious the two were head over heels about each other.

Hope looked around for a quiet escape and caught Sinclair watching her from across the tent. How did he manage to zero in on her every time she felt overwhelmed?

He cocked his head in question, as if to ask if she was okay.

No, but she gave him an encouraging wave anyway.

Hope moved on to greet a couple of girls she hadn't seen since high school. After laughter and hugs, she finally relaxed into a folding chair and went about the business of catching up with old friends.

Sinclair milled with guests, but his temper hadn't cooled. He'd had it with Ryan. Watching him snub Hope was the last straw. He'd been patient, he'd tried to give his brother time and space, but really, did the whole world have to stop because Ryan still hurt?

The sun had set over half an hour ago, leaving behind darkening skies, and he found his brother on the other side of the pole barn staring down the driveway. Ryan twirled his keys like he contemplated an early departure. Might be better for everyone if he left.

"What's with you?"

Ryan turned and glared. "Don't start with me."

"Oh, I'm going to. You were rude to Hope."

"No. I wasn't. You weren't there."

"Come off it. I saw you walk away from her."

Sinclair heard Ryan mutter a curse. He was tempted to return the same but didn't. Instead he stepped closer. "You're not the only one in the world to feel pain, you know."

"Really, *Sin,* you think?" Sarcasm dripped from his icy tone. "Oh, wait, you're Sanctimonious Sinclair now, home to save us all."

His hackles did more than rise, they nearly sprang off his back. "You don't get it, do you? You're not alone. There's not a day that goes by that I don't wish I could take back that dare. Not a moment when I don't see her lying on the ground."

Ryan started to walk away. "I'm not talking about this."

Sinclair grabbed his brother's arm. "Maybe it's time you did."

Ryan pushed him away with both hands. "Yeah? Where were you the last three years when I wanted to talk about it?" He pushed again, hard. "Huh? Sin? Where were you!"

The sheer agony in his brother's eyes made Sinclair step back, defeated. "I'm sorry."

Ryan snorted with contempt. "You're sorry. Everybody's sorry."

Sinclair swallowed, but his throat was so dry and tight he thought he'd choke. He'd hurt so many people with his stupidity. Time was no healer when it came to Ryan. God could heal him, if Ryan would only let Him.

"It's my fault she's not here." Sinclair raked a shaking hand through his hair. "I couldn't deal with that then, so I ran away. I can't change what happened, but I'm trying my best to deal with it now."

"No." Tears welled in his brother's eyes, taking him by surprise. "The fault's mine. All mine."

Sinclair reached out to him, but Ryan walked away.

He watched his brother enter the open doors of the pole barn. Taking deep breaths didn't ease the ache in his chest. Losing his brother was like having his limbs ripped off and being left to bleed to death.

He'd seen injuries like that after the earthquake. He'd had to help choose who got care and who didn't because they were too far gone. Sometimes he had nightmares about it still.

"Jesus," he breathed. "Touch Ryan. Help him. Help me."

"Sinclair?"

"Yeah?" He turned around and saw Hope with

tears streaming down her cheeks. How much had she seen? How much had she heard?

"It's no one's fault." Her voice sounded raw with emotion. "Sara's death was an accident. I finally get that."

"Hope—" His voice cracked as he walked toward her.

She rushed forward and wrapped her arms around him.

His shoulders shook, but he held on tight to the lifeline she offered. "I'm so sorry."

"I'm sorry, too. Please forgive me."

"Aww, Hope. What for?"

"For blaming you."

He lost it then.

And Hope squeezed him tighter. She buried her head into Sinclair's neck and sobbed right along with him. She envisioned her guilt and bitter regret flowing out of her in the form of tears. And she finally believed what she'd told Sinclair. She'd let go of the grudge she'd firmly held on to.

It wasn't anyone's fault. Sara was a smart girl who did something stupid. Driving that tractor uphill had been her choice. Like Rose Marsh said, face it and move on.

She didn't know how long they stood there crying, but neither one of them let go. Sinclair's arms around her made her feel safe, like the strong ties of docking rope that gave a ship stability in a storm. She'd cried all over his shirt, leaving behind smeared mascara, but she didn't care. He didn't seem to, either.

Finally, she shifted in order to rest her chin on his shoulder. He smelled good, like spicy soap and cotton sheets dried outside on a clothesline.

He loosened his hold but didn't let go.

Hope closed her eyes. She didn't care if they stood there all night. Sinclair made lazy circles on her back with his fingertips. He lulled her into a sweet place where everything was okay. A place with no past or future, only now.

The party blared in the background. She could hear laughter and music, but both were muffled by Sinclair's warm shoulder, solid beneath her cheek. Standing in the dark shadows of the pole barn, they were pretty much out of sight from the tents. Then the band played a slow song she remembered from high school dances.

She'd always lingered on the bleachers, wishing...

"Dance with me." His lips brushed her temple.

A shiver raced down her spine. They stood too close to really dance, so they swayed, moving slow. When she felt Sinclair's hands slide toward her hips, Hope swallowed sudden panic. This wasn't about comfort anymore.

She pulled back a little and searched his face. He gave her a hint of a smile and brushed her cheek with his thumb. "Have I ever told you that you're beautiful?"

Hope pulled farther away. "No..."

"You are, Hope, inside and out."

Her head pounded with the sound of trains running at full speed through her brain. For years she'd wished he'd look at her like this. She'd wanted him to hold her, too. She'd buried her feelings for him so deep and yet, with one word, one touch, he'd called them forth. And just like Pandora's box, he'd opened the lid to her heart, and she feared she might not be able to stuff those feelings back where they belonged.

She looked anywhere but at him. "Please don't."

Sinclair watched the changes of expressions dance across Hope's pretty face. It might be dark, but he recognized fear when he saw it. Hope was afraid of him.

He let his hands drop to his sides. Had he messed up again? "Hope, I mean it—"

"It's getting late." She cut him off. "I better go."

She backed up while patting the pockets of her slip of a dress. That flirty little dress had teased him ever since he'd spotted her.

"What are you looking for?"

"My keys." Her voice sounded frantic.

"Check your front seat." She'd always left them in her car. He used to tease her about that, calling her a country bumpkin who'd never make it in the city.

Her brow cleared. "You're right. I put them under the floor mat."

He tipped his head when she frowned again. "You okay?"

That earned him a look of pure irritation. "I'm fine. I've got to get home and check on the dog. Tell your mom thanks for me, would you? I'll see you tomorrow."

Sinclair watched her book it down the driveway as if there were wild dogs nipping at her heels. Not once did she look back.

Sinclair stepped out of the shadows, but he kept his gaze fixed on her until she started her car and drove away.

"Everything all right?" His mother appeared from out of nowhere and stood next to him.

"Fine, why?"

"You and Hope were gone awhile. Now she's leaving in a rush."

They stood in a pool of light cast by the open doors of the pole barn. Crickets chirped, and their sound rang out over the background party noise.

Sinclair shrugged. "She had to go home. She wanted me to tell you thanks and good night."

"What did you do?"

"Nothing." He hadn't acted on impulse this time. Well, not fully. He'd held back when he didn't want to. He'd never wanted to kiss anyone like he'd wanted to kiss Hope tonight, but that wild look in her eyes had stopped him cold. Was she worried about her folks? Or afraid of getting involved with him? What had spooked her?

Surely she cared for him, even if just a little bit. She'd felt so right in his arms. Perfect.

"You've got makeup on your shirt." His mom flicked an accusing finger against his collar.

"Ah, yeah, I do. I guess I better change it." He gave her a broad smile and then walked toward the house.

There were some things a man didn't admit to his mother despite her questioning looks. Caring deeply for Hope Petersen was one of them.

Hope made it to church in time for worship. Slipping into her regular pew, she set down her purse and tried to focus on the song. She'd had a rough night chasing what-ifs and why-nots until finally falling asleep sometime in the wee hours of morning. She'd promised herself that heartbreak wasn't an option this time.

This time...

Could she handle another *this time?*

Throughout the song service, Hope watched Sinclair. She stared hard at the back of his head, wishing she could uncover his thoughts. She'd never forget the look in his eyes or how it felt to be held by him. Like something out of a long for-gotten dream.

She shut her eyes tight and tried to concentrate on the words of the song. She prayed for God's comfort. Could He quiet the raging of her heart?

Was Sinclair distracted this morning?

Why, God? Why indeed. Why had He brought Sinclair home to this church?

Last night she'd experienced a huge step in healing from Sara's accident. But that wasn't all it was. Could there be more? Could she finally have something real that might last with Sinclair?

At greeting time, Hope popped up to take the kids downstairs for children's church. She side-stepped, hoping for a quick exit, but there was Sinclair at the end of the pew talking to Mrs. Lar-son, and she was grilling him about scheduling a potluck.

Their gazes met and held.

Her stomach turned over.

"Morning, Hope." He pushed his glasses up the bridge of his nose.

"Pastor." It felt awkward saying it, but she needed the distance of his title and the protection it gave her.

Mrs. Larson looked from Sinclair to her and then back to Sinclair again. Her perfectly penciled eyebrows lifted.

Hope felt her cheeks blaze. "Excuse me."

Thank God, Sinclair stepped out of her way and didn't try to talk to her. Mrs. Larson made too interested an audience.

Hope corralled the youngsters, including the Cavanaugh girls, and led them toward the back of the church. Hannah liked helping with the younger kids, and Hope appreciated the assistance.

Walking down the aisle with as much dignity as she could muster, it took every ounce of willpower not to turn around and seek out a pair of hazel eyes. Was he watching her?

She moved forward, urging the kids to be quiet, but they sounded like a herd of elephants charging down the stairs to the lower level.

Downstairs, reality hit. The multipurpose room used for potluck dinners, meetings and children's church looked small and shabby. She scanned the offices that had been sectioned off with a windowed wall and locking door for privacy. The church kitchen lay to her right, and restrooms were on the left.

She couldn't risk losing the preschool or her part in it by getting involved with her minister. What if whatever was simmering between her and Sinclair didn't last? What if these leftover feelings for him weren't real?

The need for an addition, however, was real. Not only for Sundays, but in order to grow the church. Growth lay in what they offered families, which meant what they could do for their children. A youth center wouldn't pay for a summer program or lay a foundation of Christian learning like the preschool. Get that right, and the potential was limitless.

"Miss Hope?" A six-year-old boy tugged her hand.

"Yes, Keith?"

"Whadda you looking at?"

"The future."

He cocked his head and looked at the office wall where she'd been staring. "I only see a door."

Hope smiled. "Sometimes the future begins with a door that gets opened by God."

The little guy looked even more confused, making Hope laugh. "Come on, let's sing a few songs."

Last night, Sinclair had unleashed a lot of feelings. Hope wouldn't allow those feelings free rein until the preschool had been voted on. And then maybe she'd explore the possibility of dating her pastor. If he ever got around to asking her out.

Chapter Six

On Wednesday, Hope left the church for a quick lunch. She needed fresh air, even though a streak of hot and humid weather had gripped northern Michigan. It might be late June, but it felt more like late July. That morning, she'd prepared for tonight's building committee meeting held after the midweek service. She was ready. Hopefully Sinclair was, too.

Sinclair's schedule had made it tough for them to talk about anything personal, which had been fine by her. She really didn't want to revisit what had happened between them Saturday night. Besides, the intense feelings could have been one-sided, and she really didn't want to find out those feelings had been hers alone.

Monday had been Sinclair's day off, but her heart had jumped every time a door opened that day. On Tuesday he'd had a meeting with parishioners and then spent the afternoon at the hospital visiting the grandmother of one of the church families. This morning, he'd been holed up in his office on the phone or planning his Wednesday evening message.

In between day-to-day business, Sinclair had treated her like normal, as though their embrace had had no effect on him. And that was good. Great, really. They'd healed from the past and were friends again. But every time she closed her eyes, she could feel his arms around her and remembered the way he'd looked. The way he'd smelled. Hope shook her head. Sinclair had never been interested in her before, and she shouldn't expect him to be now.

She made it back to the church and tossed her uneaten half sandwich in the church's fridge. Hope slipped into the office, grateful for air-conditioning. The sight before her made her stop and watch.

Hannah Cavanaugh and her sister, Grace, sat cross-legged on the floor with Sinclair. The three of them were surrounded with crayons and construction paper, chatting like old friends. They were so busy talking about the orphanage school in Haiti where Sinclair had spent the past three years that they hadn't heard her come in.

A contemporary Christian song played over the

radio with its volume louder than she liked, but Hope didn't move. Shannon spotted her, and Hope quickly gestured for silence by placing her finger against her lips. She nodded toward the three on the carpeted floor.

Shannon smiled and went back to working on her computer.

"How old are the kids at your school?" Hannah leaned forward on her elbow as she colored in the flower she'd drawn.

"All ages. Many live at the school because they lost both their mom and dad in the big earth-quake." Sinclair's paper had cutouts of footballs and soccer balls pasted on dark blue construction paper. He'd glued baseball cards on it, too.

Where'd he get those?

Hope knew the church supplies did not include sports cards. Sinclair must have bought them on his own for the kids at the orphanage.

"What happens in a earfquake?" Grace lisped.

Sinclair looked thoughtful for a minute. Completely at ease with these two girls, he captured his knees with his arms and leaned back. "Well, the ground shakes really hard, and it makes buildings collapse and fall down. Sometimes people get hurt. Sometimes hurt real bad."

Grace's eyes bulged, and she scooted a little closer to Sinclair. "Will we have one here?"

He ruffled her hair. "No, Grace, we shouldn't have one here."

Grace noticed her then. "Miss Hope! Come and see."

Sinclair looked at her and smiled, and Hope's stomach turned over. He was a natural with people, no matter how old or young. He didn't talk down to the girls, but connected with them on their level and made them feel important.

Hope walked toward them, fearing her heart might be dangling from her sleeve. Seeing Sinclair with young children did something to her. Too easily, she could picture him as a father. That was something she'd never done before, and an unfamiliar yearning shook her.

"When did you get back?" Sinclair asked.

"A few minutes ago." She focused on the girls. She didn't dare look into his eyes. "So what are you guys doing?"

"Drawing pictures to send to children in Haiti," Hannah explained.

"See?" Grace held up her red paper with various stick people and something that looked like it might be a dog.

"Very nice."

Sinclair grabbed a manila folder lying on the floor next to him and stood. "The kids in Haiti love getting stuff from other kids. The girls made several while you were at lunch."

Hope wrinkled her nose. "They've been here that long? I'm sorry. If you were busy—"

"No, no. This was perfect timing. See?" He flipped open the folder to show her the girls' pictures, and a personal check fluttered to the floor.

They both bent down, but Hope got there first. When she spotted Sinclair's signature and then the amount of the check, she wished she hadn't grabbed it.

Handing it over, she stammered the obvious. "So you support them?"

Sinclair tucked the check into the pocket of his khakis. "Yeah, I do."

Hope's head spun. With that kind of support for the school in Haiti, would he have anything left to pledge toward the building project?

"Pastor Sinclair?" Hannah stood up. "Here's my letter, too."

Sinclair took it. "Thanks. We'll read the return letters together. How's that sound? Good?"

Both girls nodded and smiled, and then Grace wandered over to Shannon's desk, looking for something else to do.

Hope switched gears and went into teacher mode. "Let's gather these crayons and paper first. Gracie, my dear, you know where art supplies go."

"Yes, Miss Hope." Grace dragged her feet but finally helped her sister.

As the girls cleaned up, Hope looked at Sinclair. "Thank you for giving them a little taste of the mission field."

"You never know where it might lead. Maybe we should start a pen-pal effort with our teens."

Did his loyalties lie with the youth group? Hope didn't want her kids left out, the smaller kids. "We can make drawings in children's church, too. Maybe even start a coin drive."

Sinclair's face lit up. "That's a great idea. I'd love to adopt the orphanage and school in Haiti as a church, but one thing at a time, right?"

"Right." Hope fought the dread that crept into her heart. Sinclair's real vision, his passion for ministry, remained in Haiti.

At the end of the day, Hope popped her head into Sinclair's office. He'd organized his bookcase nicely, but his desk was a mess. Papers, Bibles and coffee cups littered the top. "Need anything before I leave?"

He looked up and smiled. His glasses had slid down his nose, but instead of pushing them up, he stared at her over the dark rim. "No. But thanks for asking. Will I see you tonight?"

Her pulse quickened, but disappointment followed. There was no sign of him wanting to see *her* alone. He wanted to see her in the service and meeting afterward. That was all.

"I'm working with the kids tonight, but…" Swallowing the let-down, she gave him her best Arnold Schwarzenegger impersonation. "I'll be back."

He chuckled. "Great. See you later, then."

His attention returned to the papers in front of him, and Hope kicked herself for wishing for something more. A look or gesture, anything that might give her a clue to his feelings. She thought that maybe he'd been attracted to her a little, but now—who knew? And she was making herself crazy.

Back at her desk, Hope gathered her things and waved at Judy, who looked like she planned to work late, too. "See you later tonight."

"Tell your mom hello for me." Judy smiled.

"I will."

Once home, Hope helped her mom with dinner while her dad finished up in the barn.

"How's work?" her mom asked.

"Fine."

"You're getting along with Sinclair okay?"

"Yeah." She nodded her head. "We're getting along just fine."

Her mother stopped chopping lettuce for tacos and gave her an odd look. "But?"

She'd never told her folks about Eva's engagement party, and it felt like she was hiding something important from them. From her mom. Releasing her guilt and extending forgiveness to Sinclair were huge, and yet she hadn't said a word to anyone.

"But nothing." Glancing at her mom, Hope knew Judy Graves would have filled her mother in on the building committee issues, even if they both denied it. And that was a safe subject.

Her mom waited, as usual, for her to spill. Hope always shared what upset her, but she couldn't confess her feelings for Sinclair. She was too used to hiding them. And Hope wasn't convinced that these *feelings* were not leftovers from when she was a kid.

"He still hasn't decided what project to get behind," Hope finally blurted.

"That shows growth on his part, don't you think? Sounds like he wants to be certain before committing his support."

Her mother made a good point. The old Sinclair jumped in first and thought later. How many times had Hope been caught up in the impulsiveness of the moment, only to regret the outcome? Like the time they'd floated down the river on a huge chunk of ice that had broken in half. She'd fallen in. Sinclair had managed to fish her out, but they were both nearly frozen by the time they made it home.

Fingering the scar on her lip, Hope narrowed her gaze. "Whose side are you on, anyway?"

Her mom laughed and gave her a quick squeeze. "Yours, honey. Always yours."

Her folks were lighter in spirit since they'd come home from their weekend away. Maybe they'd gotten a little closure, too.

Sinclair watched Hope pass out her spreadsheet to the rest of the building committee members. She explained the rough costs for starting up a preschool, then she reviewed data she'd previously collected from families in the area who'd shown interest in sending their kids. Her income figures were conservative, and yet, by her projections, they'd break even in about four years.

Not bad.

Really good, actually. Everything about Hope was good, and he couldn't stop thinking about her. She made him want things he wasn't ready for. Step one in the process of courting Hope was becoming a man worthy of her forgiveness. That meant doing things right and in the right order. He wanted to gain her parents' approval and clear his intentions with the board before asking Hope out. Those things took time, and patience was never his strength, but he'd do it. For her—for both of them, really.

Judy Graves stepped up and passed out the prefab building information. Sinclair had asked her to run the meeting so he could observe and listen. If he'd stop focusing on Hope, he might learn something.

He scanned the lower costs for a youth center, noting there was no income generation. They couldn't afford a larger prefab model to allow for both, so a choice had to be made. He prayed that God would reveal the best choice. The best project to get behind and lead the charge. He owed this congregation that caution.

He owed that to Hope, as well. He didn't want to hurt her.

She'd changed into jeans when she went home, but kept on the same pretty green top she'd worn in the office. He liked what she wore these days. He liked a lot of things about her.

Seemed like everything in his brain wound its way back to her. Hope might be exactly what he wanted. What he needed. She'd make an excellent partner in building a strong church. In building his life...

"Pastor, we're ready to take a vote." Judy waited for him to agree.

"Uh, yeah. Go ahead." Sitting straighter, he watched the raise of hands for each option. Split right down the middle, and he hadn't voted. He wasn't going to, either.

"Well, Sinclair. Which is it going to be?" Chuck Stillwell's eyes held a challenge.

He didn't dare look at Hope. "I'm not ready to decide, and I don't think we're ready as a group, either. Not until a real majority of us gets behind one project can we instill confidence in our congregation. It's their money we're spending."

He waited out the murmurs of agreement and disagreement as the group broke up to go home. Hope gathered up the paper coffee cups and tossed them in the trash. Like after their last meeting, she emptied the grounds from the coffeemaker and headed for the kitchen to clean the pot.

"You'll have to get behind something, Sinclair." Judy caught him watching Hope and joined him. Standing side by side, they both knew what a blow losing the preschool would be to her.

"I know."

"The congregation already approved the preschool under the previous minister."

"I know that, too. I've talked to him on the phone a few times." Sinclair valued his predecessor's opinion.

"He's a good man who will give you good advice."

"Yeah." But Sinclair worried that Chuck might pull his support if they went with the preschool. They needed his pledge to make it work, which meant cementing Chuck's buy-in before Sinclair pushed.

Judy patted his shoulder. "I pray you know what you're doing."

Sinclair smiled. "Me, too."

He chatted with a couple more committee members before joining Hope in the kitchen. She leaned against the sink and stared out the window. She'd been quiet all night. She usually was at meetings.

"You okay?"

She whirled around, disappointment clear in her eyes. "I thought you'd left."

"Not yet."

She grabbed a damp cloth and spray bottle of disinfectant and headed back toward the meeting room where they'd gathered around tables used for Sunday school. Hope sprayed down the surface and quickly wiped up coffee stains and crumbs from the cookies Judy had brought.

"Can I help?"

She shook her head and wouldn't look at him. "Almost done."

Great. She thought he was wishy-washy and afraid to make a decision. He hated appearing weak, especially in her eyes. "Hope, I have an idea for a church picnic that I need your help with."

"Yeah?" She kept wiping the same spot on the table.

He took the cloth from her hands. "You want to get dessert and discuss it?"

She didn't look like she'd agree to go. In fact, she took a step back from him. Afraid, again.

"Please?" He needed her. Needed to talk to her.

He'd been so careful around her these past couple of days. Worried that he'd get too close in the office, he'd stayed away from her. He tried to ignore the spark that had ignited between them Saturday night. Ignoring it hadn't made it go away. If anything, the pull between them had grown stronger.

He watched her wrestle with her decision, and pushed a little more. "Come on."

The way he coaxed her with that deep voice of his was impossible to resist. Hope grabbed the cloth back with a snap of disgust at her weakness. The pleading look in those hazel eyes of his made her cave. Again.

With a sigh, she said, "I'll get my purse."

"That's my girl."

She turned sharply at that. "Your girl?"

"Well, aren't you? We've been buds forever."

She rolled her eyes. *Buds.* Yeah, like she wanted that. She'd always wanted more.

They locked up the building and headed for the parking lot.

"We can take my car." Sinclair opened the door for her.

Without a word, she slipped into the passenger seat and tried to relax. It was pretty hard to do that when everything about Sinclair seemed magnified in his silly car. His shoulders spanned a little broader in the bucket seat, and his smile was a little wider.

She wondered if he smelled as good as he had Saturday night. If Sinclair wore cologne, he didn't wear much because it wasn't strong. She'd have to get pretty close to find out, and even that temptation roared louder inside Sinclair's shiny red Camaro.

"Where to?" Her voice felt thick and dry.

"The family restaurant near Northport?"

"Great. Now tell me about this picnic." She hid behind the reason he'd asked her along. The picnic was definitely a safe topic.

"I was thinking a Fourth of July picnic will do the trick."

"What trick?"

Sinclair smiled at her like she was Grace's age and clueless. "I'd like to get to know the congregation as a whole, you know, on a more personal level."

He'd been out to lunch and dinner with several of the church members. Everyone wanted to get to know him on a more personal level. A couple of single ladies their age had met with him, too—but Hope didn't think they'd gone to lunch. At least she hoped they hadn't.

"The Fourth is Monday. People might already have plans for this weekend." Her reply sounded sharper than she'd intended.

Sinclair shrugged. "It doesn't have to be a big deal. We can grill hamburgers and hot dogs at the park in town. People can come and go as they please. We can wrap up before the fireworks."

Hope had always loved watching Fourth of July fireworks. They reminded her of when she and Sara were little. Evenings past, when it'd been cold, the two of them had bundled up in blankets to cheer every boom and burst of lights overhead. Her sister's childlike enthusiasm had been sorely missed these past few years. Hope still applauded with vigor, but more in memory of her sister.

Maybe this year she could cheer for the sheer pleasure of it. Maybe she'd make new memories with Sinclair. But would they be good ones?

"You only have this Sunday to announce it," she reminded him.

"I know."

"Sounds like you have it all figured out." So what did he need her for?

"Not the details, like games and that sort of thing."

Hope pulled out a pad of paper from her purse and jotted down questions and considerations for the picnic, as well as a mock-up announcement for the bulletin.

"What's that?"

"Plans for the picnic."

Sinclair smiled. "That's one of the things I love about you. You come prepared and ready to organize."

Hope paused midsentence while writing. He'd said it off-the-cuff, maybe even in jest. She'd been called anal-retentive before, but mention of the word *love* erased every other thought in her head.

She tapped her pen against the pad of paper. What had she been writing anyway? Hope peeked through the steering wheel and noticed his speed. "You're going too fast."

He grinned. "You've told me that since we were kids."

His smile was infectious, but she remained stern. Bike riding, skiing, boating, tubing or in cars—Sinclair had always gone fast. No matter what the mode of transportation, he loved a good thrill ride. "That's because it's true."

Instead of speeding up like he used to, Sinclair slowed down. "Better?"

The look he gave her made her stomach feel like they'd gone airborne, only to land hard. "I'm just thinking of you. How would that look for Three Corner Community Church if word got around that their pastor was slapped with a speeding ticket?"

He laughed. "It'd be pretty funny."

Hope shook her head. Same old Sinclair. But he wasn't the same, not really. And neither was she.

She didn't have to succumb to his boyish charm. She had a choice. She could protect herself by leaving him alone. If only she could forget she'd ever fallen for him.

The rest of the way to the restaurant, Hope pretended to concentrate on the notes she'd written. Anything to keep from wishing for a repeat of Saturday night. What would have happened had she not left?

Once seated in a booth with their orders taken, Hope scanned her picnic list. "I think the church can provide the meat, chips and lemonade. People can bring their own dish to pass if they want to."

She felt Sinclair's hand cover her own.

"Thanks for doing this."

She stared at his tanned skin. Sinclair had warm, strong hands with a few rough calluses on his palm. And yet she'd seen how gently his fingers grazed piano keys—felt them touch her cheek.

She tried to laugh off his gratitude. "For coming with you or making my list?"

He chuckled but didn't let go of her hand. "Both."

He had lines around his eyes, and Hope realized he was under more pressure than he showed. Without thinking, she threaded her fingers through his. "How's Ryan?"

"I don't know how to reach him. Or how to help him."

"Maybe he needs to work through this on his own."

"He's had three years to work through it, and he hasn't. It's like Ryan's stuck inside his grief."

"Maybe he's buried his memories of Sara because it hurts too much to remember. Seeing you come home has to bring it all back." Hope knew how buried feelings had a way of sprouting back to life.

Sinclair squeezed her fingers. "You might be right."

Hope wished there was something more she could say or do, but the waitress brought their order of pie with ice cream. She released Sinclair and sat back.

Looking around the restaurant, she spotted her parents a couple tables over. Her heart sank when her father gave them an unwelcome glare.

"What's wrong?" Sinclair looked around and spotted them, too. He gave her parents a nod.

Her appetite spoiled, Hope pushed her plate away. How long had they been watching them? If the scowl on her father's face was any indication, it'd been a while.

"You want me to talk to them?"

Hope gave her folks a wave. No sense ignoring them. "No. It looks like they're finished."

Her parents got up to leave, and her father made a beeline for the cashier without giving them a second glance.

Hope felt her cheeks blaze at the obvious snub.

Her mom made her way to their table. "Hello, Sinclair. You'll love that peach pie. See you at home, Hope."

"Thanks, Mom." Hope peeked at Sinclair. He'd given her mom a grateful smile.

Obviously, her dad had too much in common with Ryan. He wasn't letting Sinclair off the hook from the past.

"Sorry," she whispered after her parents were outside.

"For what?"

She jerked her head toward the door. "That whole thing."

"Don't be. It's all right. I get it."

Hope nodded, but she didn't understand her father's reaction. She understood that it might be hard to let go of what happened to Sara and forgive Sinclair, but the least he could do was be civil.

They ate their pie and chatted about picnic details. Sinclair made her laugh, and she relaxed. They talked like the old friends they'd been, but it felt new and different. Sinclair listened as she told him more about herself.

By the time Sinclair pulled into the church parking lot to drop her off at her car, Hope was glad she'd gone with him. The edginess she felt around him had eased.

Until Sinclair put his Camaro in park and turned toward her. "Thanks, Hope."

"You're welcome." She held her breath. With the windows down, the warm summer breeze teased her, making her feel like they were in a world of their own. Would Sinclair talk about Saturday night? Or repeat it?

"Well, good night." His hands gripped the steering wheel.

Guess not. Hope swallowed a twinge of disappointment and opened her door. "Good night."

Walking toward her car, she told herself this was better. He was her pastor, and they worked together. Staying friends was good. It's what was best until the preschool had been voted on. But her wayward heart had never listened to what was best.

Sinclair waited until she'd started her car, and then he drove off with a quick beep of his horn and a wave.

Being friends was good.

For now.

Hope came home to a quiet house, but her folks were not in bed like she expected. They lounged in the living room, watching the end of the news on TV. "Hey."

Her father glanced at the clock. "'Bout time you came home."

Hope ignored her father's comment and headed back to the kitchen for a glass of water.

Her dad entered like a storm cloud. "I'm not even going to beat around the bush. What's going on between you and Sinclair?"

"Nothing's going on." She was old enough to make her own decisions, even if she wasn't good at it.

"You were holding hands." Her father's agitation seemed a little over the top.

"So? We were talking about Ryan—"

He held up his index finger and pointed. "When are you going to learn your lesson?"

"What are you talking about?" she ground out.

"He's always been reckless and impulsive."

"He's changed, Dad. He's grown up, like we all do. Why can't you give him a chance?"

"Because he blew them all."

"That's not fair."

"Isn't it? Look at you. You're twenty-seven and still mooning over him."

"What?" Her eyes felt like they might pop out of her head.

"Now, Jim." Her mom touched her father's arm, but he pulled way.

"He's not worth it, Hope."

"How dare you hold what happened to Sara over his head. Over mine! If you knew how much guilt he's been carrying around—" Her voice broke.

Her father's eyes softened, and so did his voice. "This has nothing to do with Sara, honey. My problem with Sinclair Marsh has always been about you. And only you."

She jerked her head back like she'd been slapped. "Me?"

"Do you know what it's like for a father to watch his lovesick daughter get her heart trampled on year after year?"

Tears filled Hope's eyes. Had she been that transparent? Did she even now act like a lovesick idiot chasing after a dream that might never come true?

Tonight, Sinclair hadn't bothered to get out of his car when he'd dropped her off. She'd wanted him to kiss her good-night, to make her feel special. She wanted so much. But she hadn't acted on those longings. Instead she'd accepted his friendship like she'd always done before.

No pain, no gain.

She glanced at her mom, who nodded agreement with her father.

"We've all been through enough heartache, Hope. How can I stand by and let you break your heart for him all over again?"

He worried for her. Both her parents did. Well, she worried, too, more than they knew.

Stepping close, she cupped her father's cheek. "It's my heart, Daddy. Mine to give away."

He ruffled her bangs. "Don't be in a hurry to give it to Sinclair. He's ignored your gift too many times. He's had too many chances."

And God help her, but she'd give him one more. "I'm older now, and I'd like to think I'm a little wiser."

Ha! Who am I trying to kid?

"Not when it comes to him. He's put stars in your eyes since you were fourteen. You've never seen him straight."

True, all true. "I'll be careful."

Her dad's eyes softened. "See that you are, or..."

"Or what?"

Her father narrowed his eyes. "I might have to break out Grandpa's old Winchester."

The image of her dad taking a shotgun to Sinclair made her laugh out loud. How would Sinclair react if he did? Maybe she'd finally get what she wanted, but not the way she wanted it. "You wouldn't."

Her dad shook his head and gave her a crooked smile. "Just be careful."

"I will. I promise." Hope had never meant anything more.

But how did she keep her heart safe until she

knew Sinclair felt something for her in return? Something real and lasting?

Commitment had never been a popular word in Sinclair's vocabulary. He might be different, mature even, but that didn't mean he was ready to settle down. Or that he'd want to settle down with her.

No gain, no pain.

Better to play it safe for everyone's sake.

Chapter Seven

Saturday, Hope went for her usual morning run. Weekends allowed for longer distance than during the week, and she enjoyed every quiet step. Running helped her pray. And sometimes she'd even heard God's soft whisper of a voice in her heart. He was pretty quiet this morning, though. Maybe her thoughts were too loud.

The sun peeked over the trees as she turned back onto the road that led home. And a car that looked like Sinclair's slowed to a stop in front of her. She gritted her teeth. *What now?*

He waved and then got out. With folded arms atop the car door, he waited for her to catch up to him. He looked cool and comfy in a pair of loose khaki shorts and a T-shirt.

She blew out a breath and stopped. Bracing her hands on her knees, she let her heart rate slow down. She'd run harder than normal this morning, and seeing Sinclair had stolen her balance.

"Hey." She gulped in air. "What are you up to?"

"I'm looking at a house. Want to go with me?"

Sweat trickled down her back as she straightened. "I'm a mess."

He reached into the back and then threw her a towel. His eyes took her in, and he smiled. "No, you're not. Come with me."

Hope wiped her face. It smelled fresh, unlike her. Then she rubbed her sweat-soaked hair and draped the terry cloth around her neck. "You always carry a stash of clean towels in your car?"

"I thought I'd head to the beach for a swim afterward. It's going to be too hot to work in the orchard."

Hope laughed. That sounded like the old Sinclair. He'd do anything to get away from the chores that came with his family's cherry farm. "How's this year's crop coming along?"

Sinclair shrugged. "Eva and Adam and my dad are giving it everything they've got to get ready for harvest. I'll help with that, but Ryan's there today. They've got enough hands."

And that explained why Sinclair wanted out of there. But not his house-hunting plans. She cocked her head. "So you're looking at houses to rent?"

"To buy."

Leaning her hip against the hood of his car, Hope's mouth dropped open as she struggled with her surprise. Buying a house was a big commitment. A lasting one. "Why?"

"Why not?"

She laughed. That was a typical Sinclair statement. But buying a house meant that he planned to stick around for a long while. Her heart flipped inside her chest, and she clutched at her neck to calm the flutters that stirred up inside.

"You coming with me or not?" His eyes challenged her to go with him. Dared her even.

And, like always, she followed. Yeah, she was real good at making decisions. Slipping into his car, she muttered, "Fine, I've got to see this house of yours."

"There's bottled water in the cooler on the backseat." He shifted into gear and tore off down the road.

While Hope helped herself to the water, Sinclair drove past her house. Not more than a mile beyond her parents' farmhouse, he pulled into a cute cottage-like home she'd always loved. Worse, she could see it clearly from her bedroom window.

She turned in her seat. "You're looking at *this* house?"

He winked. "I am."

Hope got out and looked around in a daze.

Mist from the overnight humidity hadn't burned off yet. Pockets of haze lay in the low areas, including the backyard, making the house look like something out of a fairy tale. The exterior paint was chipped, but she could easily envision it with a fresh coat of sunny yellow. And she'd add white shutters.

"Cute, huh?" He stood next to her.

"Yeah." Why would he look at something so close to where she lived?

As if he'd read her mind, he answered, "The price is right, and it's been on the market a long time."

Another car pulled into the driveway, and a middle-aged woman got out and extended her hand. "Good morning. You must be Sinclair." Then she turned to Hope. "And you're his—"

"Friend. I'm a friend." Hope's cheeks burned as she cut off the most logical guess of who the real estate agent thought she might be. She'd nearly let it slip that she was his secretary.

"This is Hope Petersen. She lives down the road," Sinclair covered the awkwardness with a grin. "Shall we?"

"Definitely." The agent bid them to follow as she unlocked the door combination and then opened it wide.

Sinclair gestured for the women to enter first.

Hope eagerly stepped inside. Hardwoods in need of refinishing covered the first floor and sunlight flooded the living room. She spotted a corner that might be a perfect fit for Grandma Marsh's piano if Sinclair ended up buying.

Hope had grown fond of listening to Sinclair's piano breaks during the week. She looked forward to listening to him play whenever he snuck out of his office to the sanctuary. The tough part was staying at her desk. The temptation to watch him play tugged hard at times.

Once she had given in and taken Hannah and Grace to listen to him late one afternoon. Sinclair had welcomed the girls onto the piano bench with him and showed them the keys. After he'd taught them "Chopsticks," his amused gaze had sought hers over the girls' heads.

Did he even want kids of his own? He'd always been such a free spirit—family life probably scared him to pieces.

Shaking off those dangerous thoughts, Hope walked on ahead of the agent, who informed Sinclair about the new energy-efficient windows and why the current owners, now retired, needed to sell. The rooms were bigger than they looked from outside, and windows were everywhere.

Peeking out the kitchen window that overlooked the backyard, Hope caught sight of a small creek in the distance and asked, "How much land?"

"Three acres."

She glanced at Sinclair, and his smile made her

stomach flip. His contemplative expression was hard to read. What was going on inside his head?

Hope hadn't eaten yet that morning, and her belly responded with a rumble. Forcing a tight lid on her mouth, she didn't ask any more questions. She continued the tour with quiet observation. This wasn't her house.

But every room they entered, Hope pictured it furnished and decorated. Worse, she kept thinking how much she wished this was her house to buy. It needed minor repairs, but with a stone fireplace, the house was downright cozy. Perfect, really. Not too big or too small.

By the time they'd walked around the property lines, Hope struggled to keep her appreciation from showing. This house had nothing to do with her. But if Sinclair didn't want it, maybe she could afford to buy it. She'd be close enough to her parents to help out as needed....

"Can we have a minute?" Sinclair spoke to the agent.

The woman gave them both a satisfied smile. "I have some calls to make from my car."

He turned toward her. "So, what do you think?"

"Of what?" Hope stalled.

"The price of tea in China." He gave her that lopsided grin that made her insides swish all over again. "The house, goofball."

"It's nice." Why was he asking her?

He laughed. "Just nice? You seemed pretty excited about it while walking through it."

Busted. "Well…yeah, it's fun to look at empty houses."

He narrowed his gaze. Hope kicked a few pebbles in the driveway. She didn't want him to see past her excuse to the dreams she'd been having about him and her together, forever. "What do *you* think?"

"I want it."

"Just like that, you want it?" She knew his modest salary. Could he afford it?

Maybe he had savings. She couldn't imagine that he'd spent much money in Haiti, but he'd shelled out a pretty hefty support check the other day.

It was none of her business what he did with his money. But he had a history of being impulsive. "Don't you want to look around a little more?"

"I've already looked at a few, and I want this one. It's close to the church and not too far from Eva's."

And me…

"It feels right." He grinned. "I'm going to make an offer and see what happens."

Her dad had called Sinclair reckless, but that's not what scared her. This house did feel right. But what if he got together with someone else and married? He'd be right down the street. Could she handle that?

A chill took hold of her, despite the sun's heat warming her back. She really needed a shower and a little distance. "I'm going home so you can take care of business."

He stepped closer. "You could stick around and catch anything I might miss. I've never bought a house before."

No way would she sit there like they were a couple. She patted his arm. "Neither have I. You're on your own with this one."

"Thanks a lot." His grin coaxed her to stay.

But she wouldn't. Not this time. Hope gave him a pert wave and headed up toward the road that led home before she could change her mind.

Walking along the quiet country road, doubts wormed into her thoughts. Was he truly settling down, or was moving out his way of not dealing with Ryan? She prayed Sinclair wasn't running again.

Sinclair made his offer with the real estate agent. If accepted, he'd get a home inspection done to make sure the place was sound. It needed work, but he'd enjoy taking his time getting it ready before moving in. Maybe he'd ask Ryan to help, if his brother could spare some time away from his own home renovations. Ryan was good at that sort of thing.

Coming home after being away so long, he was taken by surprise by the strong urge to leave the farmhouse of his childhood. He'd never wanted to get away from his family before, just the orchard and the chores that came with it.

All Sinclair knew was that he craved privacy and a place to call his own. If he wanted to sit on the back porch and stare at trees for an hour, there'd be no one to ask him why he was doing that or what was wrong.

He loved his family, but his mom's constant concern and his dad's digging questions about the past three years were beginning to wear on him. He'd told so many stories about his time in Haiti, but some of the things he'd seen didn't bear thinking about, much less repeating.

After he'd finished up with the real estate agent, Sinclair slowed down as he drove near Hope's house and pulled into the driveway. Yeah, Hope had a lot to do with his desire to buy that house. Her eyes had lit up as she'd taken in every nook and cranny. She'd touched the staircase's hardwood railing and dipped her fingers in the creek running along the property line with something close to reverence, or desire. Her reactions seemed to confirm his decision.

He spotted Hope in her backyard hanging bedsheets on the clothesline. The breeze pressed the fabric against her, and the sight stopped him from getting out of the car. With her wet hair slicked back and the faded yellow sundress she wore, Hope could have walked out of a picture from his grandmother's ancient photo album.

Hazy sunshine shone around her, making her look incredibly feminine. And inviting. Like coming home to a freshly baked apple pie on the kitchen table.

He'd met Hope in youth group when he was fifteen and she was only fourteen. He'd often wondered what thoughts rolled inside that composed head of hers. Always composed while he told her everything about his out-of-control teenaged life. He might not have admitted it back then, but she'd been one of his best friends. Hope was more than part of his history, she was part of who he'd become.

He wanted her in his future.

The Petersens' dog, Gypsy, broke the spell by announcing his presence with a high-pitched bark.

Hope turned and frowned when she saw him.

Sinclair got out, bent down and petted Gypsy's head. "You're a good dog, but you've got a big mouth."

The dog inched closer and sat on his foot, giving him a canine smile with her tongue hanging out.

Sinclair spotted bare feet in front of him and looked up into Hope's pretty gray eyes.

"How'd it go?"

He straightened, but the dog stayed put, her tail thumping on the ground. "I made an offer, and she'll let me know when she hears back from the sellers."

"So what are you doing here?"

"Are your parents around?"

Her brow furrowed even deeper. "My mom's out riding, and my dad's in town picking up feed. What's up?"

"Thought I'd invite them to the church picnic."

"I told them about it."

"What'd they say?" He wanted to ask them in person. It felt like the right thing to do.

She shrugged.

"Sinclair!" Hope's mom waved from atop a horse. She slipped out of the saddle and walked forward. Gypsy ran to her side. "What brings you here on a Saturday?"

He smiled at the surprised but not unwelcome tone in her voice. Watching the horse amble across the yard, he pointed. "Ah, he's getting away."

Teresa Petersen waved off his concern. "He's fine. He wants the tall grass."

True to her word, the horse stopped at the edge of the mowed lawn to munch the knee-high thick grass.

"Do you still ride?" Teresa's question sounded close to an invitation.

He glanced at Hope. "Not since I went with your daughter years ago."

"She doesn't ride much these days." Teresa didn't hide her disappointment.

Before Hope could rebuff her mom's words, Sinclair added, "The church keeps her pretty busy, which is why I'm here. I was hoping that you and Mr. Petersen might consider coming to our Fourth of July picnic in LeNaro at the park. After the parade, we're serving hot dogs and burgers up until the fireworks."

He jerked his head toward Hope. "It'd mean a lot if you came."

Teresa looked from her daughter back to him. "We'll think about it. I better get Dusty to the barn and put away his tack. Thanks for the invite."

"You're welcome." Sinclair turned toward Hope.

"You had to do that, didn't you?" She didn't look annoyed. Composed as usual, her expression was hard to read.

Man, he wanted to ask her out. But he couldn't date Hope without her parents' approval. Earning that approval took on a whole new urgency. "I had to."

"Don't expect much."

"Never do." He smiled.

She shook her head. "That's a crock, and you know it."

True, he expected to get everything he wanted, even if he knew better. Life might not always work out the way a person wanted it to, but he wasn't giving up. Not by a long shot. "Come to the beach with me."

Panic flew across Hope's face. "Can't."

He wouldn't press her by asking why. Besides, he shouldn't have asked. "I'll see you tomorrow then."

"Yup. See you in the morning."

The relief he detected in her eyes stung his pride. A guy could use a little encouragement.

Sunday morning, Hope noticed several new faces in the pews, including a Mexican family with three small children. Because she had never seen them before, she figured they might be migrant workers here for the summer.

At greeting time, she approached them with an extended hand. "Hi, my name's Hope."

After accepting her handshake, the father pointed to his chest. "Carlos." Then he gestured toward his lovely wife. who had dark skin and eyes. "Bonita."

They were a pleasant-looking family. The kids were all smiling. The oldest two looked to be around seven and eight, and each one had a different missing front tooth.

"Welcome. Would your children like to go with me and the other kids? We have church for them downstairs."

At the blank looks, Hope repeated the question in Spanish.

Carlos looked relieved as he touched his wife's elbow and gestured for the kids to go, but Bonita eyed her carefully.

"You can come with me and see what it's like," Hope said.

That made the woman smile. *"Sí."*

Hope shepherded the kids toward the stairs. She chatted with Bonita in Spanish the whole way and found out they were newly employed by Chuck Stillwell. Stillwell Farms provided on-site housing for its migrant workers. Carlos and Bonita had arrived for the cherry harvest and were living at his farm until the fall.

Throughout children's church, Hope carefully repeated instructions in Spanish for the benefit of Bonita's kids. Even though they spoke better English than their parents, it was still pretty broken. How brave these people were to travel so far to work in a place where they were unsure of the language.

By the end of the service, Hope had taught the Sanchez children a simple worship song. And then she taught the rest of the class the same song in Spanish. They were finishing up the Spanish version for the third time when she noticed several parents lining the walls. Church was over, and she hadn't even noticed.

When the parents clapped at the end of their song, Hope's heart swelled with pride. She watched as parishioners did their best to welcome the new family despite the language barrier. There was a lot of hand gestures and laughter that made watching so much sweeter.

Hope loved it here. These were her people, her church, and she couldn't be more pleased with the warmth they extended.

"Gracias," Bonita whispered as they prepared to leave.

Hope told her about the parade and picnic in the park the following day. She jotted down her cell phone number on a piece of paper and encouraged Bonita to call her if she had any questions or needed anything.

That earned her a hug from Bonita. *"Sí, Sí. Gracias."*

After everyone finally left, Hope went to work gathering construction paper and stuffing crayons back in their containers.

"Thank you." Sinclair stood in the doorway.

She looked up. "For what?"

"You were amazing with that family. I didn't know you were fluent in Spanish."

His compliment spread through her like warm syrup. "You saw that, huh?"

"I see everything you do here. You're the backbone of this church."

She laughed. "I don't know about that."

He walked toward her. "I do. And I don't know what I would have done if you'd have quit."

"Yeah, me neither." She thought about Eva's party and the healing that had taken place there. She'd never have gone if she'd walked away from her job.

Maybe God knew from the beginning how much she'd needed that release. How much she needed to renew Sinclair's friendship.

He stepped closer. "Hang in there with me on the building project, okay?"

She searched his face. He still hadn't decided, and she finally understood why. For once, Sinclair was not acting on impulse. Her mother was right. He truly wanted the best for their church, and that proved he had the makings of a fine pastor.

Whether she liked it or not, the congregation and even the board would likely rally around whatever project Sinclair chose to support. For now, all she could do was hope and pray that he'd pick the preschool.

"Okay," she finally said.

"Hope, I found this—oh! Sorry to interrupt." Shannon stopped at the end of the tables, her face flushed.

Hope's voice tangled in her throat even as she backed away from Sinclair.

Sinclair didn't flinch, even though the tops of his ears were red. "Nothing to interrupt. I'm going to check my messages."

Hope watched him unlock the door and disappear down the hall into his office.

"Wow, you guys really need to do something about that."

"What are you talking about?" Hope shoved the crayon containers into a wooden cubby.

"Just kiss him and get it over with already."

"Shh. Can you be any louder?" Hope clenched her teeth and glanced into the office, but Sinclair was nowhere to be seen.

Shannon giggled. "Is it that bad?"

Hope wasn't about to admit that it was worse. Way worse. "You're impossible."

Shannon only laughed harder. "So I've been told."

This time Hope chuckled. She'd heard Shannon's husband, Jake, say the same thing a hundred times. "So what did you find?"

"An earring. Looks like yours." Shannon extended her opened palm to showcase a silver hoop.

Hope touched her empty earlobe. No wonder

the kids kept whispering and laughing. She'd had the one-earring look going, pirate-style, and didn't even know it. She slid the hoop back in place. "Thanks."

"No problem. Hey, would you mind chaperoning our youth group's trip to the Cherry Festival? Something came up, and Jake's parents can't go. It's this Thursday evening."

Hope didn't have anything planned. Teenagers weren't exactly her thing, but since the church's youth were a small group, it might be fun. "Sure."

"Do you think Sinclair might be willing to go, too?"

"Go where?"

Hope looked up as Sinclair locked the office door behind him.

"Traverse City. Could you help Hope chaperone the youth outing to the Cherry Festival?"

Hope groaned. Why'd Shannon have to make it about helping her?

"I should be able to do that."

"Great. Thanks."

Sinclair turned toward Hope. "I got a voice mail from your parents."

"Oh?" Hope braced herself for bad news.

"They're coming to the church picnic."

She glanced at Shannon, and her friend's smile widened with an I-told-you-so look.

Hope nodded like the news wasn't a big deal, even though her heart raced. "Great."

"Will you lock up? I've got to run. I received another dinner invitation."

"Where to?" Hope couldn't help but ask.

Sinclair gave her a pray-for-me kind of look. "The Stillwells'."

"Have fun." Hope smiled sweetly. "Don't worry, we'll lock up."

"Thanks."

Hope watched Sinclair bound up the steps.

"Sounds like your folks might be coming around."

"Maybe." Hope locked the door to the church.

It was far too early to get excited.

Chapter Eight

Hope scooped a pile of greasy potato chips onto her plate next to a charred hot dog topped with mustard. Sheer bliss. She scanned the people lined up for a hamburger or hot dog at the grill. With half the church families in attendance, plus a dozen or so stragglers picked up from the LeNaro Fourth of July parade, Hope figured the picnic could be hailed a success.

"I think Pastor Sinclair has started a new tradition with this Fourth of July picnic." Dorrie Cavanaugh stood behind her and balanced three plates on her forearm.

"You might be right on that one." Hope reached out when one of the plates almost took a tumble. "Do you need help?"

Dorrie laughed. "I've got it. Been doing this forever."

Hope spotted Hannah and Grace ogling the dessert table.

"Thanks for keeping an eye on the girls. I don't like leaving them home, but I don't know what else to do."

Hope smiled. "They're a big help around the office."

"They love to help, especially Hannah. Sometimes she's too old for her age, you know?"

Hope nodded. She wasn't sure what had happened to the girls' dad. Dorrie didn't talk about him, and neither did her girls. He was out of the picture. Out of their lives.

"How's it going with the building project?" Dorrie munched a chip while they perused the potluck table.

"Getting there." Hope glanced at Sinclair manning the gas grill like a pro, charming everyone with a kind word or joke.

Dressed in a T-shirt, tropical print shorts and flip-flops, he didn't fit the image of a typical pastor. He looked far too young and vibrant, but that's probably what drew people to him.

Even some guys she remembered from high school popped into line. A couple of them were married with kids, but they still teased Sinclair about becoming a minister and wearing glasses to play the part. One of them dubbed him Pastor Four-Eyes. Despite the good-natured ribbing, Hope heard respect in their voices, and a couple of the guys agreed to Sinclair's challenge to come and check out a service.

Dorrie noticed where Hope's attention had wandered, and she joined in staring at Sinclair. "He's doing a good job here. The girls love him."

Hope's gut clenched. Dorrie wasn't much older than Hope, and she was very attractive. Was she interested? "Yeah. He's great."

"I think your preschool is in good hands."

Hope looked at her then. "I hope so."

Dorrie smiled and then lowered her voice. "You like him, don't you?"

"I—" Hope felt her cheeks blaze. There was no denying the truth, but she wasn't going to announce it. Stealing Sinclair's term, she managed to say in a wobbly voice, "We're buds. We grew up together."

Dorrie only grinned wider. "Yeah, right. Don't worry. Your secret is safe with me."

Not much of a secret, if it was so easy to guess. Hope gave an awkward laugh. "Thanks."

Dorrie gave her shoulder an encouraging pat. "He couldn't find a better woman than you, Hope. If he can't see that, he's not worth your time."

Hope smiled. "Thanks, Dorrie. I appreciate that."

"It's true. I better get over there before those girls touch every brownie." Dorrie headed off toward her daughters.

"Nice picnic, honey." Her mom had just come from the grill, and she gestured toward an empty picnic table. "Go grab that table, would you?"

Hope slipped onto the bench and waited for her parents. In no time, her father sat down and dug right into his food while her mom fetched them both cups of lemonade.

"Thanks for coming," Hope said.

Her father shrugged. "A little hot, but a nice day for a picnic."

Her mom settled in next to her dad and took a quick sip of her lemonade. "Mrs. Larson says Sinclair is doing a fine job."

"He is." Hope glanced at her father.

If only they'd come to a Sunday service and hear the message, then they'd know Sinclair wasn't the same reckless kid he used to be. He'd changed.

Her father didn't answer, but his gaze narrowed as he studied Sinclair. Maybe he was trying to see those changes. Maybe he'd give Sinclair another chance.

And maybe Hope was full of wishful thinking.

Judy Graves and her husband, George, joined them. After a bit of jostling to make room, Judy turned to Hope. "This picnic was a great idea."

"Not mine. Sinclair came up with it."

"Really? He said you were the brains behind it all."

"I organized the essentials. He carried all the

heavy stuff." Hope had purchased the items needed and then stored them in the church kitchen. Sinclair had delivered the goods to the park.

Judy laughed and leaned toward her father. "They make a great team, those two."

Hope held her breath. Since when had she paired them up? Had Judy been talking to her mother, or did she see what Dorrie had so easily pointed out? Hope didn't know which was worse.

"Time will tell," her father grumbled and cut off further comment by turning to talk fishing with George.

Judy gave Hope an apologetic smile. She'd tried. *Nothing more than wishful thinking.*

Hope finished her meal and then got up to toss her plate in the trash. Regardless of what her father thought, she had a picnic to help run.

She headed for the grill. "How's the supply of burger and dogs?"

Sinclair scanned the shortened line. "I think we've got enough."

She peeked inside the large cooler, revealing only a couple packages of hot dogs floating on icy water, and didn't agree. Letting the lid close with a soft click, Hope straightened. "I should make a quick run to the store."

He touched her elbow. "Don't. When they're gone, they're gone. There's potluck left to eat. Besides, we need to get the games rolling soon."

Hope nodded and looked around. "I didn't see your parents at the parade. Are they coming to the picnic?"

"Cherries are ripe. They're working in the field today." Sinclair's mouth tightened.

No wonder the Stillwells hadn't come, and Bonita's family was also a no-show. Due to the mild spring and especially warm start to summer, harvesttime had come a little early in cherry country.

Sinclair tore open a package of hot dogs with more force than necessary, and they sprang to life, bouncing onto the grill.

Hope jumped forward to catch a couple before they rolled off and hit the ground.

"Thanks." He served the few people left in line.

Something bothered him. Maybe a fight with his brother? "Everything okay?"

"Couldn't be better." He sloughed off her concern with a carefree grin and reached for the second package of dogs.

"Forget it. You'll have them in the grass." Hope sliced through one end with a small knife before handing over the opened package. "Is Ryan giving you grief?"

"No—well, maybe." He sighed. "My place is here, right?"

Hope searched his face. He had a lot of people

to please, and it wasn't his job to make everyone happy. Hadn't Judy said the very same to her?

"Of course it is. They managed before without you."

Sinclair turned the dogs. "They have, but I feel guilty not helping out. There's a lot riding on this harvest for Eva. They lost a good portion of the crop in the storm a few weeks back. I can tell she's worried."

"You can't take care of everyone and fix everything. You said so yourself."

He smiled at her. "I can try, though."

Hope took in the weariness of his eyes. Sinclair was pulled in many directions, and she didn't want to be one more responsibility on his plate. Not yet, anyway.

"What?"

"You're doing a good job as our pastor."

His eyes brightened. "You've made it easy."

Hope snorted. "I've hardly done that."

He touched her hand. "Yes, you have, but thank you for saying so. Coming from you, it means a lot."

Looking back on their friendship, she'd always been the naysayer, nixing so many of his outlandish ideas. She gave his hand a squeeze.

"Watch these, will you? I'll get the games set up."

Hope nodded. She'd help him any way she could, even if it meant grilling hot dogs.

* * *

"Great picnic, man." Jake Williams, Shannon's husband, gripped his shoulder.

"Thanks." Sinclair winced. He'd helped all morning with the cherry harvest, and his muscles weren't used to the abuse.

"They're lining up for the three-legged race. You better grab a partner."

"I'm going to pass." Sinclair was in no mood to tie his leg to someone else's.

He'd already joined the egg race and felt sticky from the summer heat that finally promised to diminish as the evening wore on. Wiping sweat from his brow with the bottom of his T-shirt, Sinclair gazed with longing at the narrow portion of Lake Leelanau, where kids splashed along the reedy shoreline.

Spying Jim and Teresa Petersen getting ready for the race, he wished he'd had the chance to talk to them. He'd greeted them at the parade, but the rest of the evening's picnic had flown by in a blur. Manning the grill had taken up most of his time.

After the three-legged race, a few innings of softball ranked as the final game. He checked his watch. Only eight o'clock. It'd be at least another two and a half hours before the sky would darken enough for fireworks. He'd almost forgotten how late the sun went down in July up here.

Grabbing a paper cup full of lemonade, Sinclair

sank into a chair, perfectly content to watch the race from the sidelines. Jake and Shannon paired up, which promised an interesting sight considering that Jake towered over his tiny wife.

"No three-legged race?" Hope approached with two wide ribbons in her hand and eagerness in her eyes.

"You really want to do this?" Sinclair squinted from the late sunshine as he looked up at her. He was a mess, with grease stains on the front of his T-shirt and sweat soaked on the back.

"Oh, come on, don't be such an old man."

He should refuse, but one look at her and his willpower was toast. "Old man, huh? I'll show you who's the old man."

He followed her silently to the starting line, and his gaze traveled the length of her. She was dressed modestly, in a pair of long shorts and a sleeveless button-down top. He still wanted to kiss her. Had ever since Eva's party. Wouldn't that make the church picnic memorable, if he planted a good one on Hope right in front of everyone?

He shook his head. There'd been a time when he wouldn't have cared, but now he did. Kissing Hope was not going to happen. Not today, at least. He had to get the image out of his head. Yeah, maybe he had turned into a fuddy-duddy old man.

At the starting line they slipped off their flip-flops and got into position. Hope pressed her leg against his. Her skin felt cool compared to the embers smoldering inside him. With their bare feet lined up, Sinclair noticed her toes.

"You painted them red, white and blue."

Hope wiggled her piggies. "Nice, huh?"

"Yeah." He really needed that jump in the lake about now.

"Let's tie up." She fumbled with the ribbon before finally binding their ankles together.

But when she rose to join their limbs above the knee, he took control by grabbing the ribbon. "Give me that."

"What's with you?" Her eyebrows rose as he pulled the ends of the ribbon with a tight jerk.

"Ouch!"

"Sorry." Sinclair loosened the knot and managed a double bow.

She shook her head. "You spent three years in Haiti, and you can't take a little northern heat?"

"It's the humidity that's killing me," he muttered.

Judy Graves blew an earsplitting whistle and then yelled, "Everyone on your mark!"

Sinclair looped his arm around Hope's trim waist. She did the same to his. He looked at her pretty face and wondered what in the world he was doing. "Ready?"

She smiled. "Uh-huh."

"Get set!" Judy hollered.

Sinclair scanned the line. It was a good thing Hope's parents were also racing so they couldn't see him pressed against their daughter. This whole thing made him crazy.

"Go!"

With a leap forward, Sinclair and Hope moved as one.

She giggled, and they faltered.

And Sinclair suddenly wanted to win. "Step with me on my count. One." He jerked her forward. She giggled again.

"Come on, Hope. Two!"

Finally, they hit their stride and gained momentum. They even passed a few people. Cheering from the sidelines deafened him, but other senses took over and distracted him. Such as the buttery scent of Hope's sunscreen.

He tightened his grip, but when his fingers brushed Hope's side, his concentration wavered. He quickly let go, just as the ribbon around their thighs loosened and slipped down to their feet, tripping them.

They were going down.

Hope's squeal of laughter echoed in his ears as he whipped her around in an attempt to keep them both upright and off the ground. He halted his steps, and she slammed into him. Her ankle was still tied to his, and she wobbled.

"Steady, Ms. Petersen." He wrapped both his

arms around her back, but resisted pulling her too close.

Her gray eyes widened as she braced both her hands against his chest.

He zeroed in on her lips. Would they taste as sweet as they looked?

"Hope and Sinclair disqualified!" Judy blew the whistle again.

"That's it then." Hope's voice sounded hoarse as she pushed away from him. "We're done."

At the sound of applause for the winning pair, Sinclair glanced at the finish line. Hope's parents came in first place, followed by a bunch of kids and then Jake and Shannon, who fell across the line laughing.

"I'm ready for a dip in the lake. How about you?" Hope bent to free their ankles.

He raked his hand through his hair. "We better get the teams ready for softball first."

Hope grinned. "I'll get the equipment from the back of your truck."

Instead of following Hope, Sinclair walked toward her parents to congratulate them. "Nice job on the win."

Teresa Petersen smiled. "Thank you, Sinclair. Did you race?"

"He paired up with Hope, but they didn't finish." Her father had obviously seen them, but Sinclair couldn't read the man's reaction.

Teresa Petersen's smiled widened a little. "What happened?"

"I didn't tie the knot tight enough. Our ribbon fell off."

"Tying the knot is the key to success." Teresa winked.

Sinclair didn't think she referenced the three-legged race. Her obvious hint at marriage triggered a twitch in the corner of his eye. Maybe he had an ally in Hope's mom. "I'll remember that."

She nodded. "Good."

When he glanced at Hope's father, his confidence weakened. If the irritated look Jim Petersen gave his wife was any indication, he wasn't too happy with Teresa's insinuation about tying the knot.

But the picnic had worked. He'd made connections with his congregation by actions instead of words, and maybe the same had happened with the Petersens. He hoped so.

Sinclair overheard Hope announce the lineup for softball. He'd concocted a sign-up sheet where folks could choose their team by picking their captain—Sinclair or Hope. He used to go to Hope's softball games in high school. She'd been pretty good.

He looked at Jim. "Are you going to play?"

Hope's dad shook his head. "I'm sitting this one

out. I twisted my knee in the three-legged race. You go ahead, Teresa."

"Not without you." She draped her arm around her husband. "Thanks for inviting us, Sinclair."

"You're always welcome. It's your church."

"It's your church now. And it looks like you're doing well by it."

"Thank you, Mrs. Petersen. I appreciate that." Sinclair could have shouted for joy.

And then he glanced at Jim. Hope's father gave him a grudgingly short nod, but it was better than nothing.

"Come on, we're starting!" Hope waved him on.

"Gotta run." Sinclair took off to join the fun.

Half an hour later, he stood ready to bat with no one on base. So far his team had no runs and Hope's had two. Shannon pitched. She'd been lobbing in balls that begged to be hit far and deep. Hope played second base, and when he glanced her way, she gave him a cheeky grin.

He hit the ball hard into left field. Running as fast as he could, he rounded first base, but Hope was bouncing at second, yelling for the shortstop to throw it to her.

The shortstop bobbled it, so Sinclair kept going toward third. He glanced to his side, and Hope ran right next to him. "What are you doing?"

"You're not going to make it," she taunted.

The shortstop threw the ball to Jake at third. Just

like Hope said, Sinclair wasn't going to make it. He skidded to a halt and then twisted and headed back to second. The shortstop was already there, covering the base. He was stuck between bases with Hope looking to tag him out.

"No way can you keep up with me," he said.

Her eyes gleamed. "Try me."

He made a dash for second, hoping Jake would overthrow the ball. But Jake tossed it to Hope, and she chased him down and slapped her mitt against his belly.

"Out!" Hope yelled.

"Show-off," he muttered, breathing hard. "You're not supposed to steal the shortstop's thunder, you know."

"I knew I could catch you." She laughed and pinched his side. "You're so out of shape."

Sinclair sputtered. "Oh, yeah, Miss Fancy-Glove. How 'bout you put your running prowess to a little race?"

"Against you?" Hope raised her eyebrows. "How about after the game?"

Still trying to catch his breath, Sinclair nodded. He remembered that she was a runner now and suddenly wished she hadn't risen to the challenge. He wasn't sure he could beat her. "Maybe. After the game."

"Okay, you two—let's get back to work." Shannon caught the ball from Hope. "We have a game to win here."

They played on. Sinclair's team scored a couple runs, but Hope's team remained ahead by one. But then Sinclair easily caught Hope's infield pop fly ball for the inning's last out.

Up to bat again, he popped up between right and center field. The outfielder played too deep, so Hope ran backward in an attempt to catch the ball, but somehow she slipped. And with a squeal, she fell. Hard.

His heart stopped when she didn't move.

Sinclair raced toward her, his pulse pumping loud enough to echo through his brain. "Hope?"

The shortstop thundered close, and Judy rushed forward from right field. But Sinclair was already there, kneeling next to her. Too scared to touch her, too scared to move her, he peered into her face. "Hope?"

Sinclair heard more people running toward them, but he concentrated on Hope lying flat on the ground with her eyes closed. "Can you hear me?"

She held up one hand gesturing him to wait, and clutched her neck with the other as she gulped for air. "I'm o-okay."

His head spun with relief as she caught her breath and managed a strangled laugh. He reached behind her shoulders and helped her sit up.

"Knocked the wind right out of me," she croaked.

He pushed back her damp, dark hair with shaking fingers. Her face glistened with perspiration. He gazed into her mirth-filled eyes. "You're all right."

She nodded.

How many times had he dragged her into something where she'd ended up getting hurt? He traced the tiny scar on her upper lip with his fingertip. He'd caught all kinds of flack from her folks for that stunt. Hope had, too.

She leaned against his shoulder. "Are you okay? You look funny."

He felt funny, too. Cupping her cheek, he smiled. "I'm fine. Now."

But he wasn't okay. It hit him like a shovel to the back of his head, stealing his sense of time and place. Their past and future blurred together as it sank in that he might be falling for his best friend.

Yeah, he was falling all right. *Hard.*

"Back off and let her breathe!" Jim Petersen's voice boomed in his ear as the man's rough hand clamped down on his shoulder.

Sinclair moved back on his haunches, but not before catching sight of Hope's parents' worried expressions. Their faces had gone pale with fear. Were they thinking of the daughter they'd lost? Sinclair knew the answer to that when he looked into Jim's eyes, filled with accusation and blame.

"I'm okay, Dad. I'm fine." Hope's voice sounded irritated by all the fuss.

Sinclair's stomach turned sour with bitter regret, and like a rewound film, the wide-awake nightmare of the tractor accident flashed before him. Ryan had barked those same words to back off and let her breathe. Back then, leaning over Sara Petersen's crushed body, Sinclair had known she wasn't going to breathe much longer.

Hope accepted her father's hand and bounced to her feet.

Sinclair backed away, his thoughts racing. He stood straight enough, but his insides wobbled and pitched as he watched the Petersens coddle their daughter. Judy Graves pushed a bottle of water into Hope's hands.

"Really, I'm fine." Hope waved them all away. Her gaze held his, and he read the apology there.

Who'd he think he was, anyway? Her folks hadn't forgiven him for Sara's death, and even if one day they did, he'd remain a constant reminder of their loss. Even though they put on a good face by coming to the picnic, it was clear they'd never accept him as the man for Hope.

Cleanup was a cinch. Hope dumped what little remained of the lemonade and gathered up leftover paper products into a basket. Everyone had already put away their potluck items in anticipation of the fireworks. Blankets and lawn chairs littered the ground as people lounged all over the park, waiting. Traffic would turn into a mad dash once the show was over.

The sun had long since set, cooling the heavy air somewhat. She tossed the basket in the back of her car and grabbed a thin cotton sweater. She felt sticky, and despite the warm evening, her arms were riddled with goose bumps.

Hope had definitely picked up some of her chill from Sinclair. He'd kept his distance since the end of the softball game. After her dad's reaction, she couldn't say that she blamed him.

She spotted Sinclair loading the gas grill into the back of a pickup with Jake's help. Sinclair had borrowed his sister's truck for the picnic. After loading in the cooler, he sat down on the opened tailgate and let his bare feet swing.

She should talk to him. When he cracked open a can of pop, she wandered over.

"Thanks for your help." Sinclair shook Jake's hand.

Jake looked at Hope and nodded. "No problem. See you around."

Hope wasn't sure what to make of the scene surrounding her fall on the ball field, but she'd never forget the fear in Sinclair's voice or the terror in his eyes. The horror on the faces of her parents, though, was what gnawed at her most, making her feel like she had to explain. But how?

"Hey." She leaned against the tailgate of the truck.

"Hey, yourself." He lifted his glasses and rubbed the bridge of his nose. Those lines were etched a little deeper at the corners of his eyes, and his nose looked sunburned.

"Guess we never got around to that swim." She smiled.

"Nope."

"We never got around to that race, either."

"Nope." He looked at her. "I'm not sure I would have beaten you."

"Really?" She made a face. "Now I know you're not the same old Sinclair."

"Why's that?"

"You'd never concede a loss. Even if I won fair and square, you'd have had an excuse."

He chuckled. "I suppose so."

"Thanks for coming to the rescue back there."

His smile looked grim. "You scared a few years off my life."

"Sorry." Is this how it'd be? Everyone freaking out because of a little tumble?

"Hope—" His cell phone rang. Looking at the caller ID, Sinclair's brows furrowed. "I have to take this."

"Should I leave?"

He shook his head, so she stayed and listened to his clipped responses to bad news. When he finished the call, he sat very still and looked stunned.

"What's wrong?"

"My cousin, the one stationed in Afghanistan, has been hurt pretty bad. A roadside bomb, and they don't know—" His voice cracked.

Hope touched his arm. "What can I do?"

"Pray." He hopped off the tailgate. "My parents are going with my aunt and uncle to a hospital in Germany. He'll be transported there. My mom wants me to drive them to the airport. I don't know how they did it, but they managed to get on a red-eye flight going out after midnight."

Hope cupped his cheek. "Be careful."

He covered her hand with his and kissed her palm. "Hope, I wish..." His gaze searched hers, but then he shook his head. "I've got to go."

Hope backed away as he slammed the tailgate shut and dashed for the driver's seat. What did he wish for? The same things as her?

Please, Lord, let it be so.

She remembered Sinclair's cousin. He was older by a few years, and both the Marsh boys had idolized him when they were teens. Sinclair's uncle Larry and aunt Jamee must be beside themselves with worry.

And she felt guilty for her lovesick petition. Just then, the first firework launched with a deep-sounding *whoosh*. Her heart heavy, Hope looked into the sky as it exploded into hundreds of glittering sparks overhead.

Was that how a roadside bomb sounded when it exploded? She rubbed her arms, feeling even more chilled than before.

Please God, not another loss.

Chapter Nine

On Thursday evening, Hope milled around the church parking lot with Shannon as parents dropped off their teenagers for the trip to Traverse City.

"Is Sinclair still planning to come?" Shannon bounced her eighteen-month-old baby girl on her hip. Her little one would be confined to a stroller most of the evening at the Cherry Festival.

"He said he'd be here." Hope scanned the parking lot, but there was no sign of Sinclair's red Camaro. "He's usually late."

Sinclair had left a note by her computer that he'd help chaperone, but it'd been three days since she'd last seen him at the church picnic. She'd spoken to him briefly on the phone a couple times, because he'd called out for the week. With his parents in Germany, his sister needed his help to bring in their cherry harvest.

The office had loomed empty without him. She

missed chatting with him over coffee and listening to him play the piano upstairs in the sanctuary. Even Dorrie's girls missed him. They showed up yesterday looking to make more pictures with Sinclair for his school in Haiti.

Hope knew from the sticky notes found every morning on her computer that Sinclair had come into the church office late at night. Harvesttime meant long days, but he still managed to email a sermon outline for her to include in Sunday's bulletin.

The first week of July was typically slow at Three Corner Community Church. Because of vacations, Wednesday night services and meetings were usually canceled, and this week was no exception. Hope used the quiet time to update the spreadsheet comparing the youth center costs with the preschool. She was more than ready for the following week's building committee meeting.

"He better get here soon—the kids are antsy." Shannon shifted her daughter and checked her cell phone for messages.

So far, they'd been waiting around for roughly fifteen minutes. Earlier, Jake had prepped the church's bright yellow bus for the half-hour drive south. The tank was full and the interior swept clean. They were ready to roll, as soon as Sinclair joined them.

Laughter caught her attention. Jake entertained

their group by juggling three small beanbag balls. Nobody looked antsy to her. Not yet, anyway.

"Good. There he is." Shannon pointed.

Hope spotted Sinclair's car coming down the road at lightning speed. He quickly turned into the parking lot with a squeal of tires that made everyone stop and stare. She shook her head. Some things about Sinclair hadn't changed. Maybe they never would.

The erratic beating of her pulse made Hope think some things hadn't changed much about her, either. Her stomach took a dive when he trotted toward them. Without his glasses, dressed in shorts and a golf shirt, Sinclair looked young and carefree. His skin gleamed with a suntan from working outside all week, and his slicked-back hair was still damp from the shower.

He'd obviously rushed to get here. "Sorry I'm late."

Shannon grinned. "You're lucky we didn't leave without you."

"Yeah, thanks." He turned toward her. "Hello, Hope."

"I'll get the kids on the bus," Shannon said.

Hope vaguely heard her friend and coworker. She couldn't look away from the tired man standing in front of her. "You could have called and canceled tonight."

He grinned. "Not a chance. I need some fun."

Hope glanced at the busload of noisy teens totaling a baker's dozen. "Fun?"

"With you, it will be." He gently pushed her forward with his hand at the small of her back.

That small gesture, coupled with his softly spoken words, tumbled her insides. "How's your cousin?"

"Touch and go there for a while, but he's finally stable."

Hope stopped. "How are your aunt and uncle holding up?"

"They're tough, but I'm glad my folks are there with them just the same."

"Have you talked to them?" Hope wondered when Sinclair would have found the time.

"They call around midnight. It's seven in the morning the next day there."

Then he worked all day in the hot sun and yet still managed to keep up with his obligations for church. He'd even returned a few phone calls, she'd discovered. "You must be beat."

"I'm okay."

"You two coming?" Shannon poked her head out of a lowered bus window.

"Yep, we are." Hope hurried onto the bus.

The backseats were filled, so she slipped behind the driver's seat. Leaning against the window, she stretched out her legs on the vinyl bench. It'd been ages since she'd ridden a school bus.

"Way to hog the whole seat." Sinclair stopped in the aisle and gave her a look that said *scoot over*.

Tempting, but she wasn't scooting over. Her fingers itched to smooth the worry from his brow and touch that damp hair. A little physical space might be a good thing. "Find your own spot. I can watch the kids and still chat with Shannon."

"Fine. I'll just move along." He headed for the back of the bus and sat next to Chuck Stillwell's fourteen-year-old son, Jeremy.

In less time than it took to pull out of the parking lot, teen boys had surrounded their young pastor. Talking sports and joking about the picnic's softball game, Sinclair looked completely at ease. Even the girls listened to him, between whispers and giggles.

Obviously, they thought their pastor was cute. He was. Every single woman at church gave him a second glance, even though he hadn't gravitated toward anyone.

Just me. But they were only friends.

Sinclair still had enough kid in him to be a natural with teenagers. His youth center wasn't such a bad idea, really; it's just that the timing was all wrong.

"You're glaring." Shannon's voice intruded on her thoughts.

Hope laughed. "I'm thinking about the building project."

"And?"

Hope shrugged. "What if I'm wrong?"

Shannon fed her daughter with a bottle and rocked her gently. "That's why there's a committee to make the right decision. You just keep praying for direction, and God will come through."

Hope nodded. She'd been praying specifically for a preschool for so long. Had she lost sight of seeking God's plan for their church? Hope had her own vision, but did it line up with God's? Or Sinclair's, if he had one?

She glanced back at Sinclair, and his gaze caught hers and held. If only she knew what project he'd get behind. What decision he'd finally make.

Sinclair was more than ready to get off the bus when they reached Traverse City. Between the long ride and the constant chatter, his head throbbed. He'd meant what he'd told Hope. She was the only reason he didn't call and cancel tonight. He'd missed her.

Before exiting the bus, Jake went over the ground rules with everyone. He verified that each kid had Shannon's cell phone number as well as Hope's. After they agreed on a time and place to meet, they charged down the steps and moved as a group across the parking lot toward the ticket booth of the festival.

As far as cities went, Traverse City was small, with an undeniable sense of tight community. The Cherry Festival exemplified that with cherry pit spitting, cherry pie eating contests and a festival beauty pageant for local girls. Traverse City held many fairs, but the weeklong Cherry Festival was one of the largest and drew crowds from all over the Midwest.

Parades, air shows over Grand Traverse Bay, arts and crafts and food were all part of the fun, but their main purpose for coming lay in the amusement rides and carnival games. Jake and Shannon took a few kids who wanted to walk around, while Sinclair and Hope headed for the midway with a group that was anxious to get in line.

"It's been ages since I've been to one of these. How about you?" Sinclair breathed in the smells of grilled brats and popcorn wafting from the food arena while their charges dashed ahead.

"I was here last year."

"With the youth group?"

She shook her head. "No."

Sinclair's interest piqued. "Who, then?"

"Jake's brother, Chris." Hope's cheeks looked rosy.

Sinclair didn't like the idea of her sharing this experience with someone else. Pretty stupid for him to assume she wouldn't have had boyfriends, but the Hope he remembered hadn't gone out much. Even in college, he couldn't recall Hope ever talking about someone special in her life. He put on a neutral face and lightened his tone. "A date, huh?"

"Shannon set me up when Chris came for a visit."

"How'd that go?"

She laughed. "Not well at all."

The sudden urge to pound the guy's face surprised him. "Why? What happened?"

"I don't know which was worse, having nothing to talk about or watching him check out every woman under the age of fifty."

"He's an idiot."

She patted his arm. "Thanks, but I've never been a head turner."

"Says who?" Was she nuts? With her smooth skin and gray eyes fringed with dark lashes, she was beautiful.

"You never looked." Her voice was barely above a whisper.

He studied her closely. Okay, that was true back in the day, but not now. Now, she had the type of beauty that a man only needed a couple of long looks to appreciate before it drove him crazy.

He cleared his throat. "Good thing, too. I'd coaxed you into enough trouble."

"True." She laughed. "Remember the last time we *berged* the river?"

"Floating on that block of ice? Oh, yeah." He'd never forget that one.

He'd come home from Bible college for spring break with a few friends, and he'd talked Hope into going with them. Honoring the insane spring tradition, they'd cut a huge section of ice from Lake Leelanau with a chainsaw and then set up lawn chairs and their coolers and stripped off their shirts to catch some sun while they floated. It'd been too warm that year, and partway down river, their "iceberg" had cracked in half. Hope had fallen in.

"I thought your parents were going to kill me when I brought you home half-frozen."

Hope jostled his shoulder. "I'd never seen you so shaken up before."

"Your lips were blue." Sinclair noticed that a group of their kids were walking toward them.

"Pastor Marsh, we're headed for the Ferris wheel," one of the girls said. The rest of the kids had already scattered.

"We'll meet you in front of the welcome center at nine." He turned to Hope. "Do you want to go on any of the rides?"

"Nothing too fast."

He chuckled. "Then what's the point?"

"Not getting sick."

He laughed again. "Come on, I'm sure we can find something tame enough, even for you."

She stuck out her tongue, but followed him along the midway.

They rode the Ferris wheel and then the swings, but Hope looked a little pale when they finally got off.

"How about some games?"

Hope pressed a hand to her stomach. "Yes, please."

Sinclair shook his head. "You're so weak."

"Weak? I'll show you who's weak." She glared at him and then stomped up to a game booth set up for a milk bottle toss. "I'll take two sets of five balls. One for me, and one for my friend here."

"I'm not throwing." Sinclair stepped back to watch. His shoulders were shot from harvesting cherries. Way too much lifting.

"Fine." Hope purchased her own set and then gave him the extra softballs to hold. She stretched her arms and shoulders, and then launched a ball toward the old-style glass milk bottles.

The first ball missed and hit the canvas tarp behind.

"Nice form." He winked at her.

Her cheeks turned pink, as he'd intended. But then she grabbed another ball and threw. It hit hard, dead center, and knocked down every bottle.

"We have a winner!" the man in charge announced over a cheesy sound system. "Pick your prize, young lady, or three dollars more gets you the chance for the big bear."

"I'll take the T-shirt." Hope turned and grinned at Sinclair before picking a white T-shirt with last year's Cherry Festival logo on it.

"It's not even current."

She shrugged. "I don't care. It'll make a good sleep shirt."

He gave her a long look, and then finally muttered, "Must be the practice you got at the picnic."

"Must be." She gave him a cheeky grin.

Sinclair handed her the prize and their fingers skimmed against each other.

"When are we going to race?" Hope tipped her head.

"I don't know if I can risk it."

She laughed then. "Are you really afraid you'll lose?"

"Maybe I am. Or maybe I'm afraid you'll get hurt. Seems like I have that effect on you." He'd been afraid of a lot of things after she'd fallen hard on her back playing softball—these new feelings for her being one of them.

The last thing he wanted to do was hurt her.

Her eyes widened as if he'd hit a nerve. Or maybe she was thinking of her parents' reaction. Whatever it was, a weird tension hung in the air between them.

One step at a time.

That had become his motto.

He leaned close to her, close enough to smell the clean scent of her hair. "Now what?"

She moved away from him. "I'd really like an ice-cream cone."

"Let's go then." Catching up to her, his fingers brushed hers, so he took her hand. Warmth pooled in his belly when she laced her fingers through his, and he gave them a squeeze.

There couldn't be any harm in enjoying the feel of her hand in his, even though this was starting to seem more and more like a date. He still hadn't talked to her parents about permission to ask out their daughter. After the picnic incident, he feared they'd tell him to get lost.

At the ice-cream stand, he watched Hope scan the chalkboard that listed the flavors. She wore another pair of long shorts and a fitted peach-colored T-shirt. He'd never seen her look prettier as she studied that board.

And like a tourist, she ordered a scoop of Traverse City cherry ice cream. He screwed up his face with distaste. "Nice choice," he said sarcastically.

"I happen to like cherries."

He'd had his fill of them growing up. "Since I forgot my glasses, will you tell me what flavors they have in chocolate?"

Hope rattled off a few varieties.

"I'll take the triple chocolate fudge."

"Nice choice." Hope copied his tone. "The only thing more boring than chocolate is vanilla."

"You calling me boring?"

She laughed, then tipped her head as if considering. "That's one thing you've never been."

"Is that good or bad?"

"Oh, no, that's good." Hope looked away because their order was ready. The way her cheeks flushed confirmed her compliment, making him feel as if she'd given him a badge of honor.

With cones in hand, they found a wooden bench seat under a large maple tree, away from the heavy foot traffic. Sinclair waited for Hope to sit down before he scooted in next to her. She settled her tiny purse and T-shirt prize between them like drawing a line in the sand. He didn't appreciate the boundary, even if it was there for his own good.

A comfortable silence settled over them as they ate their ice cream and watched the people go by. And then Hope sat up straighter, as if suddenly remembering something. "You never told me what happened with the house."

"After a couple counteroffers, I got it."

"Really? When will you move in?"

He shrugged. "I'm supposed to close in three weeks, but we'll see how it goes."

"We'll be neighbors."

"Yeah." He wanted way more than that, but obviously God was teaching him patience. Like now, waiting for Hope to finish her ice cream. He'd polished off his in no time, and Hope's cone was dripping all over.

"You need help." He scooted closer and took a bite of her ice cream.

"Hey!" she protested.

"It's melting." He took another bite at the same time she licked the other side, and their noses touched.

Looking into her surprised eyes, Sinclair recalled his latest vow not to rush.

Breathe and count to ten.

But Hope quickly sat back and wiped her mouth with a napkin. She looked so flustered and pretty. Sinclair leaned forward. "You missed a spot right…here." He touched his lips to hers.

When she didn't respond, Sinclair pulled back and searched her face. Hope looked madder than a honeybee taken off its blossom. "Sorry, but I thought—"

"Did you know that you were my very first kiss?" No, she wasn't mad, but her expression warned him not to mess with her. She had shadows in her pretty gray eyes—shadows that said remembering that first kiss was painful.

Snipe hunting!

He'd hurt her with that stunt. All those years ago, when he'd joked about the way she'd kissed him, he'd done a number on her. But he'd been blind to her then. Now he could see.

"Let me be your last," he whispered.

Her eyes widened.

She didn't believe him…so he kissed her again.

Through a hazy, dreamy kind of fog, Hope heard giggles and then a whistle. She quickly broke away from Sinclair.

"Way to go, Pastor Marsh!" Jeremy Stillwell gave them a mischievous grin. And that led to more ribbing from the four boys standing in front of them.

Hope slid a little farther down the bench, wishing she could disappear.

"Okay, guys, that'll do. That'll do." Sinclair checked his watch. "It's almost nine. Let's head for the welcome center."

Hope gathered her purse and T-shirt in an effort to calm her insides. Her ice-cream cone, or what was left of it anyway, lay on the ground. She'd dropped it when he'd kissed her. And then she'd wrapped her arms around him and kissed him back.

"I'm sorry." Sinclair offered her his hand.

Hope ignored it and stood on her own. She

didn't want him to feel how much she was shaking inside. "Don't worry about it. No big deal."

That was the lie of the century. She briefly closed her eyes. She'd been so close to admitting her feelings. So very, very close.

His hand slipped to the small of her back. That point of contact radiated heat through her now frozen body.

Her breath caught. Had she heard him right?

"You okay?" He whispered close to her ear.

She nodded vigorously, but any minute her knees might give way or she'd break down in tears. Neither was acceptable, so she kept walking forward.

"Wait 'till I tell the rest of the guys," Jeremy Stillwell taunted. He rushed ahead, eager to spread the news of what he'd interrupted.

Hope cringed. It was only a couple of kisses. Deep, drawn out, reach-the-depths-of-one's-soul kind of kisses, but still. How bad could it have looked?

Her face flushed. It couldn't have looked good. She and Sinclair had been caught kissing in public. On a youth group outing, no less. Her stomach turned over, as though she'd been on those swings a few too many times.

When they reached the welcome center to meet up with the rest of the group, the kids wouldn't let it go. The boys whistled again, and the girls giggled and then launched into that K-I-S-S-I-N-G song from elementary school.

"That's enough!" Shannon scolded.

Hope's ears burned, and her face flushed hot. But her lips still felt deliciously swollen. She glanced at Sinclair. The back of his neck looked red.

Shannon gave her a wide-eyed look that begged for details.

Hope shrugged. Did everything between her and Sinclair have to be rolled up in regret?

Jake clapped a hand on Sinclair's shoulder, stalling him. "Everyone, load up."

They headed for the bus, which was parked nearby. The kids ran ahead. Fighting the desire to turn and run in the opposite direction, Hope trudged alongside Shannon, whose daughter lay zonked out in the stroller. Jake and Sinclair lagged behind.

"I think Jake's giving him an earful."

Great. Hope briefly closed her eyes. She didn't need a protective big brother right now.

"This keeps getting better and better," Hope muttered.

Shannon smiled. "It'll be okay."

"I hope you're right."

By the time she climbed on the bus and sat down, Hope wanted to fade into the green vinyl.

When Sinclair stepped down the aisle, he

slipped in next to her. Giving her a weak smile, he wrapped his hand around hers. "It'll be fine."

She didn't know how he could say that in light of their terrific lack of judgment. He was the pastor, and she worked for him. The board was bound to disapprove when they found out.

The kids continued singing that stupid song.

She jerked her head behind them. "Maybe you should sit back there and keep them quiet."

He gave her fingers a light squeeze. "You sure you're okay?"

"Now that I'm sitting down, I'll be fine."

He gave her an odd look.

She tried for some levity. "My legs are over-cooked spaghetti."

He smiled. "Nice side effect."

The kids clapped when Sinclair joined them and proceeded to tease him about when they were getting married.

Hope's stomach turned over again. "Okay, knock it off," Sinclair growled.

Hope didn't dare slide down in her seat, but oh, how she wanted to.

"Let this be a lesson to each of you. Think twice before kissing in public."

The kids laughed, and Hope gripped her temples. Another kiss made into a joke!

* * *

He'd blown it again.

Once back at the church parking lot, Sinclair watched Hope dash for her car minutes after saying good-bye to the group. Why couldn't he have waited until they were alone, on a real date? He might have jeopardized that, too.

Jake had had every right to lecture him about putting Hope in this embarrassing position. To his credit, Jake worried more about Hope's feelings than the example they'd failed to provide the youth group. Sinclair had damage control to do, which meant talking to each of these kids' parents.

Raking his fingers through his hair, Sinclair took a deep breath and approached the car belonging to the most busybody of all church gossips.

Mary Stillwell.

"Jeremy, can you give me a minute with your mom?" Draping his arm on the roof of the champagne-colored sedan, Sinclair leaned down to talk to Mary.

"You gonna kiss her, too?" Jeremy snickered.

"Cool it, buddy. Wait by Jake until I'm done here." He glanced at Mary, whose eyes had gone round as bus tires. He'd just yelled at her boy.

"What's this all about, *Pastor?*"

Sinclair didn't miss the emphasis she placed on

his title. The Stillwells had a way of making him feel like he was playing church. And not very well.

"Tonight at the festival…" This was like confessing before a school principal. "The kids saw me kiss Hope Petersen. I wanted to let you know before things got blown out of proportion."

Mary surprised him with a smile that said he'd finally done something smart instead of stupid. "I didn't know you two were dating."

"We're not." Sinclair realized how bad that must sound. "I mean, not yet."

Mary's eyes hardened. "Well, for Hope's sake, I hope you figure it out." She craned her neck and hollered. "Jeremy, get in the car!"

Sinclair stepped back. He'd only made matters worse with that botched confession. Looking around the parking lot, dread skittered up his spine. He'd messed up good by not following the right order of things, and no doubt the board would hear about it. Everyone would hear about it.

He ran a hand through his hair, wanting to pull some of it out. Under his breath he chanted, "One parent down, several more to go."

Chapter Ten

"Aren't you going to work?" Hope's mom poked her head around the bedroom door.

"I don't know." Hope snuggled deeper under the covers with a groan.

The bed shifted as her mother sat next to her. Brushing fingers through Hope's hair, she asked, "Are you sick?"

"Maybe."

"Is this about kissing Sinclair?"

Hope sneaked a peek at her mother, who looked as calm as Lake Leelanau on a hot summer day. "How'd you know?"

"Mary Stillwell called me last night, after she'd picked up Jeremy."

Hope groaned again. "Why can't everyone leave it alone?"

"Mary was concerned about you and thought I should know."

"Yeah, right." Mary loved news. Especially something this juicy to pass along.

Her mom chuckled. "Mary said that Sinclair told her about it first because he didn't want things blown out of proportion."

What did *that* mean? Was Sinclair sorry he'd kissed her, or was he worried this might cause a scandal at church?

"I wonder if he talked to all the parents." Hope didn't envy Sinclair for that one.

"Sounds like he did. I got another call this morning."

Hope smashed the pillow against her face. At this rate, the whole church would know about their very public display of affection. How was she supposed to face the phone calls today? How was she supposed to face *him?*

Her mom pulled the pillow away. "Don't be so hard on yourself."

Didn't her mother understand how these things could spin out of control? "What if this causes problems for Sinclair as the pastor, or the board sees a problem with us working together?"

Her mom touched her arm and smiled. "Oh, honey, people in love do crazy things sometimes. I'm sure every parent Sinclair talked to understands that. The board will, too."

This was exactly what her father had warned against. Embarrassment and heartache, and maybe even the loss of her job—all because she'd fallen under Sinclair's spell yet again.

Only that wasn't fair. This wasn't Sinclair's fault. Instead of cutting their embrace short like she should have, she'd returned his kiss with every dream about the two of them she'd ever had.

"I wonder if Dad will understand?" Hope whispered.

"He will. Eventually. I'm going to invite Sinclair for dinner Sunday. You two can't go back now, so you might as well move forward." Her mom patted Hope's leg, still tucked under the sheets, and rose to leave.

Her mother was right. She couldn't hide her feelings anymore. Now was the time to find out if Sinclair meant what he'd said about wanting to be the last man she ever kissed. And if he meant it, then what were they going to do about it?

Her mother hesitated in the doorway. "You've done nothing wrong, Hope. Don't forget that."

"I know." Hiding at home was not an option. With Sinclair still out of the office, she'd only have to face Shannon, who'd pump her for details, and Judy.

Judy would definitely have something to say about it if she knew. Hope should probably tell her. With a sigh, Hope threw the covers back and sat up. She might as well deal with the fallout from last night sooner rather than later.

"That's my girl. I've made your favorite chocolate chip muffins."

A muffin couldn't fix this, but she appreciated the effort and smiled anyway. "Thanks, Mom."

Hope headed for the bathroom to take a quick shower, and her mom's words echoed through her thoughts.

People in love...

Were they really in love? She'd loved Sinclair for so long. These feelings were nothing new. Trying *not* to hide them was terrifyingly new and different. She'd never felt so exposed. Vulnerable.

Driving to work, she couldn't stop thinking about Sinclair talking to all those parents. She could easily picture him pulling his hair in frustration. Caring about what those parents thought proved how much he'd changed.

Entering the office, Hope glanced at her desk and groaned. The message light on her phone blinked. She dropped her purse and reached for the play button, but hesitated. Coffee first.

Even as she scooped fragrant grounds into the filter, the familiar scent of promised caffeine didn't soothe. Her gaze continually strayed back to that phone blinking with evil abandon. She headed toward it with itchy fingers and finally hit the speaker button.

Sinclair's deep voice played clearly over the chugging of the coffeemaker. "Morning, Hope.

You're picking up my bad habits. You're late. I'll try you at home." After a pause, he added, "Man, I miss you."

Her heart tumbled, and she smiled.

The door opened and Judy Graves hurried inside, juggling her purse and hand-stitched, quilted briefcase. She was also later than normal.

"Morning, Judy." Hope held her breath. Did she know?

Judy smiled. "Do you have a minute?"

Ugh. She already knew. "Yep."

"Get yourself a coffee first." Judy went into her office and then poked her head back out. "Can you bring me one, too?"

"Sure." Hope fixed two cups and then made her way toward Judy's office. Thinking about the kids' stories being told about her and Sinclair made her cheeks blaze.

"Oh, Hope," Judy said as she took a cup from her. "You're head over heels in love with him, aren't you?"

Hope squared her shoulders. "You heard about last night."

"Yes. Sinclair called me."

"Really." Hope's stomach fluttered. Sinclair had tried to nip inevitable gossip in the bud by calling first. That was a good thing. It showed he cared. She plunked into a chair and rested her mug of coffee on Judy's desk.

"I got his call right before Mary Stillwell's." Judy gave her a weak, disappointed kind of smile.

Her hopes deflated. This was about damage control. "I see."

"I'm not sure that you do. Your relationship with Sinclair is under the microscope now. The whole church is watching, looking for you to set a good example. Dating a pastor is different. It has to be."

"I know that." Did Judy think she had no sense? She knew they had to be careful. Even if they hadn't been at the Cherry Festival.

Hope had worked at the church for years. She'd never willingly jeopardize her job. Or Sinclair's.

Judy gave her a pointed look. "You need to be *really* careful. Don't ever be alone in the office."

Hope's cheeks flared hotter as she wrapped her hands around her mug of coffee. "Of course not."

Judy reached across her desk and touched Hope's wrist. "You okay?"

Hope looked at Judy, not as a board member and boss, but as a friend. "Mom's invited Sinclair for dinner Sunday after church."

Judy's eyebrows rose. "Are they coming for the service?"

"I don't know yet. I hope so. I think they're trying, you know? For my sake."

Judy nodded. "That's good. Don't let them down, Hope. Don't let any of us down."

"I won't." Hope knew exactly what she meant.

Running her fingertip over the tiny scar above her lip, Hope silently vowed to keep that promise.

Saturday afternoon, Sinclair slipped his cell phone into his pocket after leaving a message on Hope's voice mail. He'd already confirmed his dinner invitation at the Petersen home with Hope's mom yesterday.

Still, he wanted to talk to Hope. Needed to talk to her. See her. They'd been playing phone tag since Friday. He downed a bottle of icy-cold water while waiting with his brother for Eva to bring back lunch. Adam had gone to help her. They'd spent a hard morning in the orchard.

"Problems?" Ryan slipped onto the picnic table.

"No." They'd made a silent truce this week, but that didn't mean they could talk like they used to.

Sinclair needed to wait until after dinner with the Petersens before making any plans with Hope. Again, God's lesson in patience was hammering inside his head.

"Thanks for taking time off to help with the harvest this week." Ryan cracked open his second bottle of water. "It means a lot to Eva."

"Yeah, sure." Sinclair hopped onto the top of the picnic table next to his brother.

He stared out over the fields he'd grown up hating. They didn't seem like a trap anymore.

Working in the orchard had brought them all together again.

Ryan couldn't take time off from work because his position as the farm manager for a horticultural research station that specialized in cherries made it impossible for him to walk away from his own duties at such a peak time. But he helped out where he could, and so did Eva's friend and roommate. Beth manned a block of sweet cherry trees that Eva opened up for public picking.

Sinclair nodded toward the higher part of the orchard. "Did you see that family in the U-Pick block?"

Ryan laughed. "Those kids wore more cherries than they picked."

"You should have seen how fast they were shoveling cherries into their mouths. I'm guessing a bellyache's on tap for later."

Ryan nodded.

"Eva's struck gold with the U-Pick," Sinclair said.

"What's up with you and Hope?"

Sinclair shrugged off his surprise at Ryan's direct question. "Why?"

"I heard you got caught kissing at the Cherry Festival."

Tomorrow morning's service promised to be interesting, considering the gossip buzz flying around enough that even his brother knew. "Who told you?"

"I ran into Jake Williams at the gas station."

"Nice." Sinclair took another swig of his water.

"Are you serious about her?" His brother had never looked so stern, and that said something, considering Ryan always looked stern.

"I think so."

"Don't go there unless you're certain."

"I'm certain, okay?" Sinclair understood Ryan's protectiveness, but he'd been whipped enough. Judy had lectured him pretty good.

He got that the Petersens had been through a lot. They didn't want Hope to get hurt. No one wanted Hope to get hurt, including him. Sinclair wouldn't break her heart for anything, but how did a guy promise not to ever do that?

He kicked the dirt off his boots against the picnic table seat. "I'm having dinner there tomorrow."

Ryan laughed.

Glad for the sound, Sinclair smiled, too. "What?"

"Get ready for Jim's interrogation."

Sinclair knew he'd have to come clean about his feelings for Hope if he expected her parents to trust him. What worried him was how they'd get beyond what had happened to Sara. Could Hope's parents let that go, or would it linger forever between them?

Sinclair saw the chance for Ryan to open up. "Did he grill you?"

Ryan couldn't tread water forever, keeping his memories buried deep below the surface. A ghost of a smile curved his brother's mouth, but dark sorrow shone from his eyes. "Yeah, Jim grilled me big-time. Especially before I took Sara to the prom."

"Who'd you ask first, Sara or her dad?" Sinclair meant way more than the dance, and hoped his brother understood where he wanted to go.

Where he would go, when the timing was right.

Judy had warned him not to rush into anything. She'd told him that Hope deserved to be courted and fussed over, and Sinclair would do his best to honor that request. Hope deserved the best he could give her.

Ryan diverted the conversation away from himself. "Hope's been crazy about you since we were kids."

"I was stupid then." Sinclair noticed Eva and Adam approaching with lunch.

Ryan gave him a hard look. "Don't be stupid now."

Sinclair nodded. Good advice, but not much help.

On Sunday afternoon, Sinclair stood on the side porch of the Petersens' farmhouse. Adjusting the tuck of his shirt into the khakis he wore, he hesitated before opening the screen door.

"They won't bite." Hope pushed him forward.

"They might." Sinclair opened the door and went inside.

He and Hope had survived the church service despite the number of smirks and winks they'd received. News about their kiss had traveled fast through the congregation.

When he'd first spotted Jim and Teresa Petersen slide into the fourth-row pew, Sinclair wasn't sure whether to feel relieved or be scared to death. Jim wore a scowl the entire service that warned him to be careful with his daughter or else.

Fortunately, Jim hadn't balked when he'd offered for Hope to ride home with him after church. That had to be a good sign. The threat of rain had kept their dinner party indoors instead of the planned cookout, but once the smell of pot roast hit him, Sinclair was glad. Roast beef was one of his favorites.

"Have a seat. Dinner is almost ready." Teresa, decked out in an apron, waved a big knife toward a chair at the table.

He wasn't going to argue with that knife. Sinclair sat down at the long oak table in the kitchen, feeling strangely at home and out of place at the same time. He hadn't been in the Petersens' house in ages, but it hadn't changed. The kitchen wallpaper was still the same, and the lacy curtains were identical to the ones he remembered.

"Mr. Petersen." Sinclair rubbed his palms against the tops of his thighs. He sat across from Hope's father, who looked at ease sipping his iced tea. "Thank you for coming to service this morning."

He glanced back at Hope as she helped her mother. She'd kicked off her sandals and roamed the kitchen barefoot. Watching her graceful moves stirred a sharp longing to have her puttering around the kitchen with him, in the home he'd just purchased. Would she be surprised to find out that he'd learned to cook?

"Nice message this morning." Jim Petersen fiddled with his butter knife.

Floored by the compliment, Sinclair wondered if Jim's reason for giving it was to divert his attention. "Thanks."

"How do you like pastoring a church?"

Sinclair cocked his head. "The responsibility is intimidating."

That answer pleased Hope's father, if the lifting of the scowl was any indication. "Judy says you're doing a fine job."

As long as he handled dating Hope properly.

"Dinner is ready." Teresa Petersen set a platter of fragrant beef and warm biscuits on the table.

Hope followed with bowls of fresh vegetables

and whipped potatoes. A heavy meal for a summer day, but Sinclair couldn't wait to dig in.

"What do you want to drink? Iced tea or pop?" She grazed his shoulder.

Sinclair nearly jumped at Hope's touch. "Iced tea is fine."

Pretty hard to relax when he had no clue what to expect from her father. They were obviously trying to be nice to him, but tension hung like a rope in the air. Sinclair didn't want to hang himself with it when he read the warning in Jim's eyes.

"Hope tells me that you bought that little cottage down the road." Teresa ladled a generous portion of pot roast onto his plate before handing it to him.

"I'm waiting for the financing approval, and then I can close and move in. If you ever need a hand with anything, let me know."

Jim shared a look with his wife. Sinclair wondered if he'd said the wrong thing. Considering what happened the last time he'd helped bring in hay for the Petersens, they might not want him anywhere near their farm.

Or their daughter.

Rubbing the back of his neck, he couldn't ease the tightness that had settled there.

"We'd appreciate that." Teresa sat down next to her husband.

After a brief prayer, everyone concentrated on

the business of filling and then emptying their plates. Conversation bounced like a beach ball from how many heads of cattle the Petersens had this year to Sinclair's duties in Haiti.

Finally, when dinner had ended, Sinclair rose from the table to take his dish to the sink. He spotted Gypsy on her bed in the corner, waiting for scraps.

Hope intercepted him. "I've got this. Go on in the living room while Mom and I get dessert ready."

"I thought we might walk a bit." Jim Petersen headed for the screen door.

Sinclair searched Hope's face, and she gave him an encouraging smile.

Turning toward her dad, he pushed up his glasses and his palms broke into a sweat. This is what he'd come for. "Lead the way."

He followed Jim out the door. Peering at the darkening sky, Sinclair knew the rain wasn't far off. Thunder rumbled low in the distance, and he swallowed. This was the grilling Ryan had warned him about.

Walking along the gravel driveway, Sinclair wondered if he should talk first or wait for Jim to take the lead. Sinclair knew what he wanted, but what was the protocol here?

As they approached the barn, Sinclair's heart

sank when Jim opened the main doors where he'd kept his tractors parked. Why were they going in?

Sinclair stared at the old John Deere—the one that had crushed Sara—and his gut tightened.

"There's something you need to know." Jim's eyes looked glossy, and his voice sounded tight.

Sinclair braced himself against the emotions clogging his throat, threatening to choke him. "What's that, Mr. Petersen?"

"I never blamed you for what happened to Sara. I don't blame anyone but her."

Sinclair let out his breath as relief flooded through him. He didn't know how to respond so he remained quiet, but he nodded for Hope's dad to continue.

"Sara had a wild hair that liked to drive too fast and take chances. Even as a baby, after learning to walk, she had to climb instead."

Jim smiled, remembering. "She wouldn't let me put training wheels on her bicycle, no matter how many scrapes she got from falling over. She wanted to do things her way."

"Sounds a lot like me." Sinclair had often found a thrill-seeking partner in Sara when they were teens. When Ryan hadn't held her back.

Jim nodded. "Your brother curbed that wildness in her. I thought she'd matured in college and left a lot of her silliness behind. You dared her to do something she'd probably already tried on her own. I know it was an accident, Sinclair. A stupid one."

Sinclair stared at the man in front of him, knowing how hard it was for him to say what he had. It didn't make their loss any easier, but the tearing guilt eased. They could move on from here.

Sinclair searched Jim's eyes and finally, with a thick voice, he said an inadequate "Thank you."

Jim slapped a work-hardened hand on his shoulder. "My problem with you is Hope."

"Sir?" Sinclair swallowed hard.

"What's this business of kissing her while you're chaperoning a group of kids?"

He ran a hand through his hair and watched as the first few drops of rain hit the dusty path in front of the barn. That metallic scent of a summer shower filled his nostrils. "Not a wise decision."

"No. Not at all. Just what are you up to?"

"Up to?"

What would he do if Jim sent him packing? He wasn't giving up Hope, not now. Not when he knew he needed her and wanted her in his life forever.

Jim shook his head. "Do I have to spell it out? What are your intentions? Are you dating my daughter for the fun of it, or what?"

"I'm not dating her yet, sir." He couldn't help pointing that out.

"Oh, yeah? You've taken her out for dessert, for lunch even."

"All work related. Mr. Petersen, I want to go out with Hope. Not because I don't already know she's right for me, but because I want to do this the right way. And that means asking you first."

Jim smiled. "Asking me what?"

Sinclair clenched and unclenched his jaw. This wasn't coming out as smoothly as he'd planned. "If I can date your daughter."

"Why?" The man enjoyed making him miserable.

"Because I'm crazy about her!" There, he'd finally said it out loud. He liked the way it sounded, too. His heart felt warm and squishy inside. He'd never felt like this about anyone before.

"Is that so?"

"Yes, sir." Sinclair's irritation dissolved when he realized that Jim wasn't going to stand in their way. He was being a dad. And a good one, at that.

"When are you going to let her in on how you feel?"

Sinclair thought about it for a moment. Hope deserved more than impulsive snipe-hunting stunts and stolen kisses at a fair.

He understood what Judy meant about not rushing their relationship. He knew exactly what he needed to do.

With a broad smile, Sinclair said, "When the time's right."

Chapter Eleven

Hope stared at her reflection in the mirror. Jeans and a T-shirt might be casual for her first real date with Sinclair, but they were going for a horseback ride. She plunked onto the edge of her bed and pulled on socks and her boots.

Yesterday's rain had broken the heat wave that had gripped the area. It had also prevented her and Sinclair from taking a walk. Soon after he'd come in from the barn with her father, they'd eaten dessert and then Sinclair had left. He'd asked her out after she walked him to the door, while they stood on the porch saying good-bye.

He wouldn't give up any details regarding his chat with her father, though. Her father had been equally obtuse, but evidently he was satisfied that Sinclair meant her no harm. Tonight's date proved that much.

Hope smiled.

"Hope!" her mom called up the stairs. "Sinclair's here."

"I'll be right down!" Hope hollered back. She gave her reflection another glance and figured she'd do.

Tromping into the kitchen, she stopped cold when she spotted Sinclair holding a huge florist's bouquet of mixed flowers. Warmth spread through her. "For me?"

He smiled. "For you."

She took the bundle and buried her face in the petals. Breathing in scents of rose and lily and the tangy perfume of daisies, she whispered, "They're gorgeous."

His gaze caressed her. "So are you."

She stepped closer and soaked in every detail of the man who'd finally asked her out. "Thank you."

Her mother cleared her throat as she set a water-filled vase on the table with a clunk.

Hope laughed. She'd forgotten her mom was in the room. Evidently Sinclair had, too, because his face flushed red under that scrumptious tan of his.

"How was your day off?" Hope arranged her flowers in the vase. He'd called her at work that day only to confirm their date and suggest they go riding. "Were you in the orchard?"

"A little. My parents flew back from Germany. I picked them up this afternoon."

Hope sobered. "How's your cousin?"

"Stable. My aunt and uncle will stay with him until he's transferred to a VA hospital in the States. Ready?"

"Yes." A shiver trickled up Hope's spine. She'd waited a long time for this. She turned to her mom at the sink washing pots and pans from dinner. "We'll be back before dark."

"Be careful."

Hope glanced at Sinclair and smiled. "We will."

Walking to the barn, Hope glanced again at Sinclair. She'd known him forever, and yet she couldn't seem to put two words together.

He smiled.

She smiled back.

Silently, they entered the barn with its familiar smell of grain and warm horseflesh. Her horse, Sonny, nickered softly. She'd brought the horses into their stalls before dinner and lined up the tack to save time. All they needed to do was saddle up and go.

When Sinclair looked a little lost, she asked, "Do you remember how to do this?"

"Saddle up or ride?"

"Both."

He grinned at her. "Watch me."

That wouldn't be hard. He wore jeans and a T-shirt, too. She liked the way his muscles flexed as he swung the saddle onto the horse's back. He straightened the saddle pad underneath and then tightened the girth strap.

"You've got to watch Dusty. He bloats his belly. Give that strap another couple pulls to the next hole."

Sinclair nodded and yanked the girth strap higher. The horse groaned, shifted his weight and stomped a foot. "I don't think he likes this."

"He's fine. He wants to stay in the barn, and this is his way of trying to do that. He'll get oats after we come back." Hope struggled to tighten her horse's girth strap.

"Here, let me."

She felt the warmth of him as his arms came around either side of her. "I could get out of the way, you know."

"I kind of like you right where you are." His lips brushed her ear.

The smell of leather and Sinclair's spicy scent teased her senses. She let her head fall back against his shoulder. "I do, too."

He kissed the side of her neck and whispered, "We better get moving."

"You started it."

He chuckled. "Okay, true. Now get out of the way, and I'll cinch this strap.

Hope stepped back and watched him closely. Had he also talked to Judy about being careful?

Sinclair seemed hesitant, almost reserved, and that wasn't like him. At least, it never used to be.

After they'd mounted up, they headed for the twisting paths that led toward Lake Michigan. The air smelled sweet from the previous day's cooling rain, and Hope couldn't be happier. The horses, once they realized they were in for a pretty decent ride, settled down and eased along amiably. Even Dusty stopped trying to turn back for the barn.

After a couple miles, Hope shifted in her saddle. It'd been a while since she'd last ridden. "Are you going to tell me what you and my father talked about yesterday?"

"Curiosity killed the cat." He chuckled softly.

"Come on, you two were out there for ages." And Hope had been pacing the whole time.

He sighed. "At first we talked about what happened to Sara. Your dad doesn't blame me, so that's a huge relief."

"I'm glad he told you that."

"Me, too."

"And?"

Sinclair grinned. "And nothing. I asked for permission to take you out. Which he obviously granted."

Hope smiled. "Obviously."

"So let's just enjoy this, okay?"

"Fine." She got the hint. Don't worry about their future. Stay in the moment. For now.

"Good." Sinclair grinned at her, and then he urged his horse into a canter and took off toward the beach.

Hope laughed and followed. He'd be sore tomorrow. They both would, but it was worth it to ride like they used to—without a care in the world.

When they reached Lake Michigan, the evening sun lay shrouded behind a bank of clouds lazing in the western sky.

Hope pointed toward the horizon. "We're not going to get a good sunset."

"We get plenty of good ones." Sinclair dismounted, looped his reins around one hand and held the other one out to her. "Come on, let's walk."

Hope followed suit, and threaded her fingers through his. They walked a vacant stretch of sandy shoreline with their horses trailing behind. "Thanks for suggesting this, and thanks for the flowers. Especially the flowers."

"You're welcome." He brought the back of her hand to his lips for a swift kiss and then stopped to pull her close.

Waves lapped the shoreline, and the horses' tails swished against their backs. Looking into Sinclair's intent face, Hope wanted more than now. Her heart overflowed with her feelings. She loved him so much.

Should she tell him?

He dipped his chin to rest his forehead against hers. "I let the board know that I'd asked you out."

"Yeah?" Hope swallowed a sudden flutter of nerves. "We'll be under the microscope now, won't we?"

He nodded. "Are you ready for it?"

After releasing a deep breath, she laced her arms around his neck. "Are you?"

He gave her that crooked smile that made her stomach flip. "I'm not playing games, Hope—"

She touched her fingertips against his lips, even though her heart threatened to explode. "I'm not, either."

Sinclair hinted at forever, and Hope battled the urge to suggest they run away right now and make it legal. She'd promised not to let her parents or the church down. And she didn't want any regrets.

"One step at a time." He nipped at her finger. "We have to take this one step at a time."

Hope had yearned for dates, late-night phone calls and the anticipation of seeing him again and again since she was a teenager. She shouldn't squander those with a declaration of love given too soon. He was right. They needed to settle into a strong relationship before taking that next step.

She sighed. "You're going to make us do this right, aren't you?"

Her horse shook and then chose that moment to rub his face along her back and side, pushing her even closer against Sinclair. "There goes my clean shirt."

He tightened his grip around her waist. "You're not making this any easier, you know."

She met Sinclair's hazel eyes, which gleamed with an intensity that gave her goose bumps, and pulled back. "Sorry."

"I don't want any regrets between us."

She didn't either, but she sort of wished for a little of the old Sinclair who'd jump first and think later.

Hope looked up as Sinclair refilled his coffee mug for the fourth time. When he turned and smiled at her, she smiled back, hoping the increased speed of her heartbeats couldn't be heard.

They'd agreed to maintain a professional distance at work, but she hadn't counted on the challenge that presented. Her fingers itched to brush back his hair that stuck out in places as if he'd tried to pull it out.

Considering that she'd transferred a call to him from Chuck Stillwell fifteen minutes ago, it was no wonder Sinclair looked rattled. He'd received several phone calls from board members this week, and Judy had spent the better part of the morning holed up with him in his office.

Could be about the upcoming building committee meeting, but she wrestled with the panicky feeling that the calls had something to do with her. Would they survive this dating scrutiny?

"Ready for tonight's meeting?" Sinclair stood next to her chair, holding coffee in one hand while the other gently rubbed her shoulder.

She nodded. "I emailed you and the committee members a spreadsheet comparison that I prepared last week. Have you looked at it?"

He leaned close. "I'll check it out."

And she leaned away from him, away from the temptation to snuggle closer. "And then maybe you'll tell me which way you're voting?"

"I'll let you know at the meeting." He gave her a playful wink, but his hazel eyes didn't hold any clues. He'd dodged the same question last night over dinner.

She watched him walk back to his office and sighed. Why wouldn't he tell her?

Shannon shook her head.

"What?" Hope asked.

"There's like this magnetic force field around the two of you that's downright sickening." But she smiled. "Fact is, I'm a little envious."

Hope laughed. "Sorry."

"Judy said she saw you at dinner in Traverse City last night."

Hope frowned. "I wonder why she didn't say hello."

"Maybe she didn't want to interrupt." Shannon wiggled her eyebrows.

Hope's stomach took a dive. Last night Sinclair had taken her to a very romantic restaurant. They'd sat side by side in a secluded booth with candlelight. In two days they'd gone out twice, which seemed promising, but Sinclair applied the brakes every chance he could. Maybe he didn't feel the same urgency as her. The same desire to make their relationship permanent.

"Don't worry, he's crazy about you."

Hope started at Shannon's words. Were her fears that easy to read? "I hope so."

Concentrating on work hadn't been easy this week. Every movement Sinclair made in the office distracted her. And now she had to wait for tonight's meeting to find out if he'd back her preschool.

What if he truly wanted a youth center? What then?

By the time Sinclair skipped down the steps leading to the church's lower level, he wished the building committee meeting done and over before it had even started. He'd had his fill of explaining his relationship with Hope. He understood the board's concerns with him dating one of his staff, but he'd assured them that he and Hope were serious. He didn't think that statement made them feel any better, though.

Last night, saying good night at her parents' doorstep had torn him in two. He'd driven past the house he'd bought, impatient to share it with Hope. But he'd promised himself and the board that he'd proceed with control and maturity where Hope was concerned. He was a pastor now, and he had to act like one—whatever that meant. He was still figuring it out.

He'd declined Hope's invitation to grab dinner before midweek service because he needed some distance so he could concentrate. His message notes had to be reviewed, and he didn't want to let slip which project he supported. She'd hear his decision along with the rest of the committee.

"Here we go again, right, Sinclair?" Chuck Stillwell slapped him on the back. He harangued him more than Hope trying to find out which project he'd support.

"I trust you've given my advice some thought?"

"I gave it a lot of thought." Sinclair took a seat at the four long tables that had been pushed together.

Waiting for the others to gather round after grabbing coffee and cookies, Sinclair glanced out the office windows toward the parking lot. Jeremy Stillwell played basketball with a couple other kids, and Sinclair wished he was out there with them.

"Holding up okay?" Hope slid into the seat next to him. She set down her file, pen and notepad for taking meeting minutes.

"Yeah, why?"

She shrugged. "You look like you've had a tough day."

He reached for her hand and squeezed. She'd worked at this church and knew these people well enough to know he'd been under some thumbs today. She'd make the perfect pastor's wife.

The apostle Paul's letters to the church at Corinth, which instructed that it's better for a man to marry, took on new meaning now. How long would they have to wait?

He glanced at Hope. With her elbows on the table, she looked ready to do battle for her pre-school. He prayed it wouldn't come to that. "You're prepared."

Her eyes narrowed. "I've waited a long time for this."

She'd waited a long time for him, too.

"What?" he asked.

"Nothing." She'd know soon.

"I'd like to call this meeting to order," Judy Graves announced.

The murmurs of separate conversations died down while everyone took their seats.

"I think we should make a decision tonight. We've kicked this project around long enough." Chuck Stillwell led the charge.

"I second that." A board member who agreed

with almost everything Chuck said raised his hand to make a motion.

The fate of the project rested on eight shoulders, and Sinclair didn't want a divided vote.

"Very well." Judy held up her copy of Hope's spreadsheet. "Have you all reviewed the comparison?"

Questions ricocheted off the group. Judy answered some, and Hope responded to others.

Sinclair listened. As much as he hated to admit it, Chuck was right. Now was the time to decide or forget the whole project. Back and forth, the debate waged until it finally died into silence.

"Well, shall we move to a vote?" Judy glanced at him.

"One minute." Sinclair sat forward. He glanced at the faces surrounding the table. Eager eyes rested on him. He read apprehension and worry in Hope's face. He finally felt worthy of her trust, and he wasn't going to let her down.

"I'm new and young and inexperienced, but I'm smart enough to recognize that families with young children are gravitating to this church."

He took a quick sip of his water before going on. "This committee had their homework done before I arrived. You've already agreed on the project to pursue, and I believe we should reinstate that. A preschool will satisfy our mission statement to grow and support this community with

God's word. Early education gives us the perfect tool to do that."

Applause erupted from several of the committee members, including Judy.

"Now just hold on." Chuck threw up his arms. "Aren't we missing the obvious here?"

Sinclair narrowed his gaze. "What's that?"

"Your change of heart has everything to do with who you're dating. You proposed the youth center when you interviewed."

"I had ideas, Chuck. Cost-effective ones, but now that I've been here awhile, I think—"

"You've only been here a month," Chuck challenged.

Sinclair looked at the rest of the committee members. Most were board members, and they stared at him in tense silence, waiting for an answer. No doubt eager to see how he'd handle open opposition.

He took a calming breath. "I've spoken with your previous minister several times about this project. This was his vision for the church, and the congregation agreed. I needed my own confirmation of that vision before I decided which way to go."

"And your confirmation came before or after you kissed our office manager?" Chuck's droll tone carried a hint of sarcasm, but his meaning was clear. Very clear.

Sinclair almost flew out of his chair, but Hope's hand on his arm stopped him. He pushed his glasses up the bridge of his nose and made eye contact with every single person around that table. "Hope and I are dating, but our relationship has nothing to do with the fact that she's *qualified* to run a preschool."

Chuck looked amused. "All I'm saying is, should we follow your *heart* in this decision? I'd prefer our votes to come from a more logical place."

Sinclair breathed in the tension of the room. He heard Hope shift in her seat next to him. He had to get this right, and that meant not wiping the sneer off Stillwell's face.

"I believe God speaks through men's hearts."

The group concurred with murmurs of agreement.

"Chuck, you and I are no different in wanting to see someone we care about realize their calling. We're not ready to support a youth pastor when our regular attending teens are less than a handful. Will we eventually get there? I believe so."

The silence was deafening, but he kept going. "Hope's proven her ability with the kids' Sunday and Wednesday night programs, and she's proven there's interest within the community for a tuition-based preschool and summer program. She's worked hard on this project. No one can deny that."

"We're busting at the seams down here," Sonja, a retired teacher and children's church volunteer, added.

Chuck squared his shoulders. "We're not denying Hope's ability or her integrity—"

"Then don't deny God's plan because of me, or your lack of trust in my integrity."

"Are you saying you've heard from God on this, Sinclair?" Judy's question pushed him to the wall.

"God established this plan before I came here. Talking to your previous minister makes that pretty clear. I'm confident this decision is the right one. You all have to search your own hearts and decide from there."

"Hope, you've worked on this from the beginning," Judy pointed out. "If we agree to move on the preschool, what is our next step?"

Sinclair could have hugged Judy for asking the perfect question to get them moving toward a positive vote. He finally looked at Hope, and his chest swelled at the pride shining from her eyes.

An instant later, Hope became all business. "I think we need to revisit the original pledges, confirm them and also open it up for newcomers to be a part of this. Before we can update our bids, we need to nail down the financing. Pledges are a big part of that."

Judy nodded and stood tall, as if daring anyone else to voice an issue. "If no one else has any questions, I propose we go to a vote."

"I second that," Sonja called out.

Sinclair looked around the table before his gaze settled back on Hope. She twisted a napkin with her fingers.

"With a show of hands, all in favor of the preschool?" Judy counted off a majority vote, but Chuck had not raised his hand. "Then it's a go."

Sinclair rubbed the back of his neck. A major hurdle overcome, but would this come together without Stillwell's support?

Hope leaned against the railing outside the church office while Sinclair remained inside chatting with lingering board members. She needed air, big-time. Judy wasn't kidding about being under the microscope. Chuck's comments about her as the reason for Sinclair's change of heart wiggled deep in her belly like a worm in dirt. Was Sinclair doing this for her or because he truly believed in the preschool?

"Good job in there, Hope. You handled yourself well." Sonja gave her a hug.

"Thanks."

"Don't you worry about ol' Chuck. He'll come around."

Hope nodded, but the implications gnawed at her. What if he didn't? Chuck Stillwell was the largest financial contributor for the project. If he pulled back his pledge...

Committee members poured out of the church and gathered up their kids from the basketball court at the far end of the parking lot. Hope said her good-nights and thank-yous even as doubts swamped her. Did any of them believe she'd manipulated Sinclair's decision?

She stared at the fields beyond the parking lot and waited for Sinclair to lock up the building. Big fat rolls of recently cut hay dotted the sloping landscape. The late evening sun cast a golden haze over everything, making it look surreal, like a scene from the past.

She wondered what the church's founding members had in mind for this building a hundred years ago. There hadn't been one addition since. Could the church rally around a big construction project?

Hope felt a warm hand touch her back.

"You okay?" Sinclair's voice was low and sweet next to her ear.

She leaned against his chest, loving the protective feel of his arms circling her waist. "Yeah. I'm fine."

"I'm sorry about Chuck."

She turned around to face him. "Don't apologize for him or anyone."

"Thanks for holding me accountable in there before I came unglued." He threaded his fingers through her short hair. "What he said isn't true."

Looking into his eyes, Hope believed him. But Sinclair didn't have her passion for the preschool. Maybe she expected too much. His calling was different from hers, but still, shouldn't he have a little more fire for the project? "What if he pulls his financial support?"

Sinclair rested his forehead against hers. "Then we'll figure it out."

Hope didn't ask how, knowing it might mean years of delay. Chuck's pledged donation was huge. They'd look at the numbers tomorrow and make a plan for the congregation to confirm their earlier pledges and make new ones. Then they'd have a better feel for where they were. Her dreams inched closer but still dangled out of reach.

Wrapping her arms around Sinclair's middle more tightly, she gave him a squeeze.

"What's that for?"

"Thank you for voting for the preschool."

He kissed the end of her nose. "Want to go somewhere and celebrate?"

They may have won the first round, but the match loomed too uncertain for a victory dance just yet.

"Honestly, I'm beat. Maybe tomorrow?" Hope gave him a brave smile.

"I'll hold you to that." He leaned close and kissed her.

Hope pulled back before he deepened it.

"What? What's wrong?"

She cocked her head toward their surroundings. "The microscope, remember?"

"I'm really not digging this whole microscope thing." He caressed her cheek. "Talk to me, Hope. Tell me what's on your mind."

"I'm fine." She took a step back. "Really. Just tired."

She couldn't describe the unsettled feelings churning inside her and couldn't quite verbalize the worry that gnawed at her gut. They were so close. Her preschool had finally received a majority vote, but Chuck's digging in for the youth center soured the success.

Sinclair ran his finger along her jaw. "Okay, we'll talk in the morning."

"Yes, we will. See you tomorrow." She gave him a quick peck on the cheek and stepped away before she unloaded her fears. Sinclair didn't need that.

With a wave, she trotted toward her car. After she'd slipped behind the wheel, Hope noticed that Sinclair stood staring out at the same hayfield. And he didn't look a bit certain of the future, either.

That scared her.

Chapter Twelve

"We've got a problem." Sinclair looked across his desk at the woman he loved, knowing he was about to deliver a huge blow.

"What's that?"

He pushed Chuck Stillwell's original pledge card Hope's way and then watched her eyes grow wide as she read it.

"No..."

"Our numbers are way off."

"But—let me see the spreadsheet." Hope pulled the papers toward her. As she stared, tears gathered in her eyes, making Sinclair feel helpless.

"I transposed the amount from the very beginning," Hope whispered.

"I'm sorry I didn't catch it before." He'd never reviewed the original pledges until this morning. He'd based everything off the spreadsheet of pledged income and construction costs approved by the board the first time around.

"What can we do?" Her gray eyes pleaded.

Sinclair covered her hand with his. "We have to revise the pledge income and see where we are."

She pulled back, away from him. "That's a huge difference. A giant mistake. My mistake."

"We have to try." It was his responsibility to make sure he had all the facts, and he hadn't done it. He'd rushed ahead.

"Are those the pledges from people who don't attend anymore?" She pointed to the short stack of cards near his phone.

Sinclair nodded. "The figure's pretty low. Fortunately, the folks that left after your minister retired were not big givers."

"You're our minister now, Sinclair." Her response was fierce, reminding him that this was his problem. His decision. His future.

Running her fingers through her hair, she blinked fast in what looked like an effort to keep it together. She continued, "And I'd already pulled them out of our figures, but I never thought to recheck the standing pledges."

Sinclair couldn't stand it anymore. Forget professional distance. He circled his desk and gathered Hope into his arms. "It's okay."

"No, it's not. I don't make these kinds of mistakes." She buried her head in his shoulder.

He held her close and kissed the top of her head. "Everyone makes mistakes."

"Not this big."

He rubbed her back, but a hug and a kiss wouldn't make it better. The preschool was shot unless they could afford to borrow the shortfall.

Hope pushed out of his embrace to grab a tissue from the box on his desk. "I'll revise those numbers and then let you know what I come up with."

Sinclair didn't like it when she shut him out. She didn't have to solve this alone. He couldn't do much but wait for her update. But he could pray.

A few hours later, after she'd delivered the updated figures to Sinclair and Judy, Hope sat outside on a bench beneath the crab apple tree near the pastoral office window.

Even after she'd included Sinclair's generous pledge, it wasn't enough.

She couldn't stop herself from asking how he could make such a pledge when he was buying a house. He smiled and told her that his parents had split the proceeds from the sale of the orchard with their kids. How much Sinclair had received, she didn't know. He didn't offer to tell her, either.

The comforting whirl of the office air conditioner drowned out all other sounds. Her stomach growled, but her turkey sandwich remained in the brown paper bag untouched.

She'd played with these figures for years, but Judy was the expert when it came to the finances for the church. If anyone could find a way, it'd be Judy.

She closed her eyes and prayed for a sign, something—anything—from God to confirm the project would move forward as planned. They needed this preschool. Dorrie and her girls needed the summer program even more.

"Hey."

Hope looked up at Sinclair. "How'd it go?"

He held out his hand. "Let's get some lunch."

She grabbed her bag. "I already have one."

When she didn't take his offered hand, he let it drop. "Picnic, then. Come on."

Hope followed Sinclair to his car. She slipped into the passenger seat, and the sun-heated vinyl burned through the thin cotton of her dress. Sitting on her hands, she rocked a little. Sinclair must have bad news, or he'd have said something more.

When he slid behind the wheel, Hope asked, "What did Judy say?"

"The church can't afford to borrow the difference." He started the engine and drove off toward town.

Yup. Bad news.

She remained silent for miles, mentally running through options and trying not to wallow in self-pity. The *tick-tick* of cool air pumping through his car vents didn't soothe her one bit.

Was *this* her answer to prayer? Or a challenge to find another way? There had to be a way.

"We might not be able to borrow more now, but in time, if we grow…" Sinclair's deep voice coaxed.

More waiting and wishing for something that might not happen. Dorrie had depended on her to be their voice, and she'd let them down. She'd let everyone down with that mistake. "What now?"

"Judy's going to contact the board." Sinclair pulled into the parking lot of a small deli that had been built on the crest of a hill on the other side of LeNaro.

"Do you think they'll renege on their approval?"

Turning off the car, Sinclair turned toward her. "I don't know. Judy strongly believes in pushing forward, and she'll go to bat for us, but we can't ignore the numbers. Neither will the board."

"It's my fault. Maybe I should talk to them." Did he think she'd wanted the preschool so badly that she'd subconsciously made it work on paper? Did the board?

Had she?

No. Hope had prayed hard for direction, right along with everyone else on that committee. In her heart, she knew the preschool was the right path, so why this enormous roadblock of her own making?

He tucked some of her hair behind her ear. "It doesn't matter how the mistake was made, only that an error in the accounting was found and corrected. That's all anyone needs to know."

But she'd been the one to complete those spreadsheets. They'd been reviewed and approved by others, even Sinclair. All of them had trusted her to be accurate. "What are our options?"

"Confirm the existing pledges and then fundraise."

"That'll take forever."

"If it's meant to be, God will provide." Sinclair reached for the door handle and got out.

Hope ground her teeth. That sounded too much like a cop-out. Maybe He didn't care what happened. And maybe Chuck had been right all along, that Sinclair's reason for supporting the preschool was only to make her happy.

She wanted Sinclair to believe in the preschool because it was the right course. Shouldn't he want it more than she did, if it was God's plan for their church? Where was his conviction?

Sinclair peeked into her side of the car. "You coming?"

"Yeah." Hope got out and followed Sinclair into the store.

Once inside, Sinclair ordered a steak sandwich while Hope scanned the case of cold soft drinks. A group of construction workers entered the deli and ordered lunch. She heard Sinclair tell one of them that they'd ordered the same sandwich.

"It's my favorite one they've got here," one of the guys said.

"Mine, too." Sinclair introduced himself.

"Marsh…hey, aren't you the new minister at Three Corner? Martha, my wife, read about you taking over in the Sunday paper." The oldest of the young men pumped Sinclair's outstretched hand.

"That's me. Are you looking for a church to attend?"

Hope inched forward, curious. She'd been running the announcement of Sinclair's pastoral position in the newspaper's section for church listings ever since he'd arrived. Several new people had come because of it, but not enough people to make raising money a snap with a new pledge drive.

"As a matter of fact, we are. My name's Denny Brown. I'm building a house in the area, and Martha saw your church and fell in love with it. That beautiful old structure reminds her of where she grew up out east."

"So you're a builder?" Sinclair glanced her way with an expression that said this guy was somehow important.

Hope's heart quickened as she walked toward them. What if this guy could help? What if he was the answer to her prayer?

"Residential, commercial, we do it all. We're

family owned and based out of Traverse City. Is this your wife?"

Sinclair smiled. "Not—ah, no. This is Hope Petersen, my office manager."

"Hello." Hope gripped the man's hand for a brief shake.

Sinclair's arm slipped loosely around her waist. "We'd like to build an addition for a small preschool, but we're pinched when it comes to finances."

Hope glanced at Denny. The guy's eyebrows rose only slightly, but she could tell he hadn't missed Sinclair's possessive touch. Would their relationship make any difference to newcomers? She'd never known pastors who dated. Especially ones who dated their secretaries. That microscope focused in a little closer. Frighteningly close.

"Pretty common situation." Denny gave Sinclair his business card. "Call me, and I'll see what I can do about a quote."

"Will do, and thanks." Sinclair pocketed the card, gathered up his sandwich and steered her toward the register.

"That was pretty interesting timing, don't you think?" Hope said while he paid for their purchases.

Was it a mere coincidence that they'd met a builder who might attend their church? She didn't think so.

"We'll see."

They wandered out into the hot July sun and chose a spot with a view. They settled around a picnic table shaded by a large blue-and-white striped market umbrella that flapped in the stiff breeze that blew in off Lake Michigan.

Hope ran a useless hand through her hair, trying to smooth it from the wind. "What about talking to Chuck?"

"About what?" Sinclair took a huge bite of his steak and cheese on rye.

"About my mistake, and see if he'll match the amount needed anyway."

"No." Sinclair coughed and reached for a drink of his iced tea. "No way."

"Why not?"

Sinclair laughed. "You're talking about Chuck Stillwell, right?"

Hope didn't appreciate his tone. Chuck was overbearing and hardheaded even, but the guy had a heart of gold. She'd seen the care he took with providing clean housing for his migrant workers, complete with a safe playground for their kids. "You don't think it's worth a try?"

"I don't."

"Why?"

His eyes hardened. "A host of reasons."

Why wouldn't he tell her? "Name one."

Sinclair shook his head. "Look, Chuck gave us

the amount he pledged. Let him confirm it like everyone else and leave it at that."

"You won't even consider talking to him?"

"No, I won't." He paused and then pierced her with a hard stare, like he had easy access to her thoughts. "And you're not going to, either."

Was Sinclair afraid to approach Chuck?

Hope took a bite of her turkey sandwich, but it tasted like dust in her mouth.

By the time they'd returned to the church, Sinclair knew Hope was mad at him. She clammed up when she was angry. She did the same when she was anxious. When they were kids, he could tease it out of her, but he didn't feel much like teasing today. He hated the disappointment he'd read in her eyes and the feeling that he'd lost her respect.

All because he wouldn't beg Chuck Stillwell.

But he refused to bow and scrape. He wouldn't do it. Not even for Hope.

Entering the office, he spotted Judy gathering up her briefcase. "Did you get a hold of everyone on the board?"

Judy looked at Hope standing rigid behind him and then focused her attention back on him. "Yes. They'd like to meet as soon as possible to review the corrected figures. And, ah…Chuck's threatening to pull his support unless we go with the youth center."

Hope stepped forward. "Without him, it's over."

Sinclair put his arm around Hope's shoulders, and he felt her stiffen beneath his touch. Yup, she was still mad. "We met a local builder at lunch, and I'd like to find out what he can do for us."

Judy smiled. "That'd be great. Gather as much information you can."

After Judy left, he turned to Hope. "We'll figure this out."

"How? Without Chuck, we've got nothing." She stepped away from him toward her desk.

He followed her, hating the fact that Stillwell's money meant so much to this small congregation. He gave a quick nod to Shannon, who tried to look busy.

He leaned against Hope's desk. "Maybe you need to let this go."

She gave him a scathing look. "Give up, just like that?"

"That's not what I'm saying."

"Then what are you saying, Sinclair? You've never believed in this project from the beginning. Maybe you don't care what happens." She threw her purse into her desk drawer and slammed it shut.

He had to admit she looked incredible, all worked up with her cheeks flushed and her gray eyes flashing.

He turned to Shannon and winked. "Would you give us a few minutes?"

"No problem." Shannon looked surprised at Hope's outburst and lifted a stack of stamped envelopes. "I'll take these to the mailbox."

"Thanks." He waited for her to leave before focusing back on Hope. "This project isn't yours to make happen."

Her pretty mouth opened and then shut.

"You need to give it to God and let it go."

Her eyes filled with tears.

"Will you trust me on this?" He caressed her cheek, and a tear dribbled down over his thumb.

There had to be a reason for all of this. He wasn't sure what it was or why, but a strange sense of calm had come over him after seeing Hope's mistake.

God was in control. They needed to remember that.

"I'm trying to." Her voice was barely a whisper.

He wanted to tell her how much he wanted to see her dreams come true. He wanted to tell her that he loved her and wouldn't hurt her for the world. But seeing the wary look in her eyes, the words stuck in his throat.

Instead, he leaned down and gently touched his lips to hers for a featherlight kiss. Hope stiffened at first, but after a little coaxing, she melted.

He had to tell her. "Hope—"

"Oh! Sorry." Shannon had returned from the mailbox. Couldn't she have taken a walk?

"Don't be." Hope pushed her chair back and gave him a pointed look. "This is not the place for that."

Sinclair straightened and watched Hope walk out of the office toward the ladies' room. He gave Shannon a sheepish smile. "Sorry about that."

"Trouble?" The receptionist raised an eyebrow.

"It'll blow over." But he wasn't so sure.

Because he'd rushed through the project notes and hadn't double-checked the facts, he'd failed to do his job. He'd failed the board, and he'd failed Hope.

Again.

Hope closed her eyes and listened to Sinclair playing the piano in the sanctuary. The turbulent-sounding music tugged at her heart and her will-power. He'd been up there half an hour playing one obscure song after another. At one point, she wondered if he'd made up the chords he played. The notes rang out relentlessly over her, and like waves crashing on the shoreline, they tugged at her. A rip current of emotion and sound emanated from Sinclair's fingers on those keys.

She was sorely tempted to join him, but stared at the stack of work on her desk. She could leave it, but pride had a way of anchoring her to her chair.

She wasn't caving in this time. Sinclair was right about trusting God to provide, but he had to be wrong about speaking with Chuck. Chuck might be God's way of providing. Chuck might be their answer.

For the youth center.

Chuck had dug in his heels, all because of her stupid mistake. But if he knew what had happened with the pledge, he might change his tune. It was worth a try.

But Sinclair wouldn't try. He'd dug in his heels, too, the stubborn man.

"You're awfully quiet this afternoon. Are you okay?" Shannon asked.

"I'm worried about the preschool."

"And Sinclair's worried about you." Shannon nodded toward the ceiling.

The music changed to the sweet notes of the old hymn "It Is Well with My Soul." But nothing was well for her. In fact, Sinclair's calm acceptance of the shortfall in funds grated on her.

"Miss Hope, come quick!" Grace, Dorrie's youngest daughter, burst into the office and pulled on Hope's arm. "Hannah cut her leg! You have to help her."

Hope looked into the tearstained face of the panic-stricken seven-year-old. With her best teacher voice, Hope tried to calm her down. "Take a deep breath and tell me what happened."

"Hannah was mowing the lawn and—"

Hope banged her way out of her chair and headed for the door. "Shannon, call 911, then Dorrie, and tell Sinclair in case—" She swallowed hard. "Can you keep Grace with you?"

Shannon, already on the phone, nodded and waved her away.

Hope darted out of the office. She heard Shannon rattle off the address to the emergency dispatcher all the way down the hall. Shannon's voice always rose when she was nervous.

Hope ran across the parking lot and into the hayfield that lay between the church and the mobile home where the girls lived. "Oh, God, please…"

Grasshoppers jumped in the recently cut field, hitting her arms and legs and even her face, but she kept running. Her heart beat madly, and her mouth had gone dry. Her side ached, but she continued to pray the only words that formed in her mind. *Please, Lord.*

He knew what she feared most.

Dear God, please.

As she scanned the Cavanaughs' backyard, the sweet scent of freshly cut grass turned Hope's stomach. She didn't see the little girl anywhere. "Hannah!"

Then she spotted the push mower that lay upside

down at the base of a small incline. The blades were still and the motor quiet, but no Hannah.

It was so quiet!

Frantic now, Hope rushed forward toward the mower, and then she saw a pair of small feet poking into sight behind a bush. Those feet didn't move, and one foot lay at an odd angle....

Hope clamped her hand over her mouth as bile rose in her throat. *No! God, please no.*

She dashed toward the nine-year-old, fighting back tears and nausea. Thoughts of Sara lying still underneath a huge tractor blazed through her mind. What if Hannah...

But this was only a small push mower, not a heavy tractor. *Dear God, please.*

Hope knelt beside the unconscious girl and felt Hannah's neck. A strong pulse beat beneath Hope's fingertips, but for how long? She glanced at a deep gash at the base of the girl's skinny calf, just above her ankle. Blood oozed out and soaked the grass underneath.

Hope broke out in a sweat. "Hannah? Honey, can you hear me?"

The girl stirred but didn't open her eyes. Her skin was pale and translucent looking.

Hope ripped the bottom of her skirt for a makeshift bandage. "I'm here. I'll take care of you, I promise."

She staunched the wound with the material, but

it soaked through in seconds. Hope tamped down the hysteria bubbling within her. There was so much blood!

Think! What could she do to stop the blood?

Sirens wailed in the distance, and she heard the sound of gravel crunching under tires nearby. She looked up as Sinclair got out of his car and ran toward her.

Her eyes filled with tears, and she reached a hand toward him. "I don't know what else to do."

"Is she breathing?"

"Yes. And her pulse feels strong, but I don't know—look at her foot!"

Sinclair knelt beside her, laid his hands on the girl's head and prayed. Then he looked up with haunted eyes from a face white as a sheet. Did he battle memories of Sara, too? He'd been there that day. He'd watched her die.

Hope's throat threatened to close up. "She's lost a lot of blood."

"I know." Sinclair gripped her shoulder, giving her an encouraging squeeze. "Keep praying, Hope. You did great with the bandage, and you're doing great now. Keep it together a little longer. The paramedics are on their way."

Hope nodded, glad for his assurance and the confidence emanating from him, along with the warmth of his body kneeling next to her.

The paramedics arrived as promised and quickly

took over. Hope gave them a brief explanation of what had happened and then backed away and watched. Hannah looked so small and fragile on the gurney. Her skinny little legs didn't even reach the end of the stretcher.

Hope let loose a broken sob when she felt Sinclair's strong arm loop around her waist. She couldn't let that little girl go to the hospital alone.

"I'm going with her," Hope whispered. "If she wakes up, she'll be scared."

"Yeah, and she knows you." Sinclair gave her a quick squeeze before letting go.

Hope stepped forward and told one of the EMTs, "I'm going with her." Then she climbed in before anyone could stop her.

"I'll meet you there." Sinclair hovered at the back of the ambulance.

His eyes still looked troubled, causing a chill to race up her spine. What did he know that she didn't? Hope nodded as the doors of the ambulance closed.

Hope held on to Hannah's hand while the ambulance bobbed and weaved through traffic, trying to cut short the twenty-five-minute trip to the emergency room in Traverse City. The paramedics worked fast, connecting tubes and taking vitals.

Hannah's eyes fluttered open at one point and filled with tears. "Miss Hope?"

Hope leaned closer to hear through the oxygen mask covering the little girl's mouth. "I'm here."

"Mom's going to be mad."

She laughed, giddy with relief that Hannah was coherent. There was no way that Dorrie gave her nine-year-old daughter permission to mow the lawn. Hannah would no doubt earn a lecture after this was all over. Her mother had to be insane with worry right now.

The little girl's eyes closed again as whatever the paramedics gave her kicked in and put her back under. Hope glanced at Hannah's leg, now bundled with a special splint. The blood-soaked yellow material of Hope's torn skirt dangled through one of the straps.

This should never have happened.

When they finally reached the E.R., Hope gave the nurse the information she knew. Pacing the waiting room, Hope looked up when Dorrie charged in with Grace cradled on her hip only ten minutes later.

"Where is she? Where's my baby?"

"They're looking at her now." Hope took the weeping Grace as the nurse escorted Dorrie into the examining room.

"We wanted to surprise my mom." Grace hiccupped on a sob and then cried harder.

"I know." Hope stroked the little girl's back.

Good intentions with horrible consequences. And no news. What were the doctors telling Dorrie?

Hope sat down in the overly air-conditioned waiting room and settled Grace more comfortably on her lap. She wasn't a big kid, and Hope cradled her like a toddler. As soon as she leaned back against the chair, Hope's muscles went limp, as if she'd finished running a marathon. Her head ached with worry. Would Hannah lose that foot? She'd never forget that horrific injury, with all that blood on the ground. Closing her eyes didn't help—the image came back all over again.

Hope heard the swish of the automatic doors. Sinclair rushed toward her with a concern-filled face, and something inside her broke loose. This never would have happened if they'd had the summer program in place. If only she had pushed harder before her previous minister retired.

He slipped into a chair next to her. "Any news?"

"Not yet. Dorrie's in with the doctor." Hope shook her head.

He squeezed her shoulder. "You okay?"

Hope nodded, but she couldn't keep bitterness from climbing into her voice. "With the preschool's summer program, they wouldn't have been alone."

"Hope—"

"Remember these girls' faces when you talk to the board. When you see Chuck."

This wasn't Sinclair's fault. If he felt a little of her frustration, maybe then he'd understand how desperately families like Dorrie's needed a safe place for their kids during the summer months. Maybe he'd fight harder for it. Maybe he'd talk to Chuck about his pledge.

Sinclair stood up when Dorrie came into the waiting room. Her face was pale, her cheeks wet with tears. "They need to operate. Her Achilles tendon was cut pretty bad, and they don't know—"

Hope watched Dorrie collapse against Sinclair and bawl. He held her, and then did what any good pastor would do. Sinclair gathered the four of them close and prayed.

Chapter Thirteen

Hope shut off the car's engine and leaned her forehead on the steering wheel. Tears dripped onto her bare knees. It was late. Too late to say she was sorry. Too late for an apology. It wouldn't matter because Sinclair would never forgive her.

How could he when she'd alienated the church's largest financial donor? Chuck hadn't taken her request very well. Not well at all.

Her head pounded, but the rest of her felt numb. She'd been so sure of herself after Hannah's surgery. After Hope had left the hospital, she headed straight for the Stillwells' place. She'd be so sure that once Chuck heard the circumstances behind the project's accounting error, once he heard what had happened to Dorrie's daughter, then he'd want to match the transposed pledge, and they could move forward as planned.

She couldn't have been more wrong.

Hope closed her eyes, but that sick, hollow feeling in her stomach remained. Now who was the impulsive one who acted first and thought later?

A sudden knock on the passenger-side window startled her. She straightened and spotted her dad's worried face through the glass.

Hope flipped the unlock switch.

Her dad slipped into the seat next to her. "Everything okay with Dorrie's kid?"

She nodded but didn't trust herself to speak. The doctor had said the surgery had been successful and he believed Hannah would recover fully, but it would take time and physical therapy.

"She'll be okay," Hope managed to choke out.

Her father grabbed her hand and squeezed. "You did a good job rushing to help that little girl. She needed you, and you were there. Sara would be proud."

More tears leaked out. Her dad thought this was about Sara's death. In a way, maybe it was. She hadn't been there for her sister when it mattered most.

Hope had let so many opportunities to make a difference slip by. Afraid to speak out or step up. Tonight she'd finally taken a stand and blew everything to bits.

"I ruined everything." Her voice came out scratchy and raw.

"How did you do that?"

Hope shook her head.

"What happened tonight? Did you fight with Sinclair?" Her dad's voice had an edge to it.

If only it were that simple. "No."

"He called for you over an hour ago when he couldn't get through on your cell. We didn't know where you were."

"Sorry, Daddy." She'd turned her phone off before she'd gone to Stillwell Farms.

After Dorrie was settled into her daughter's hospital room with a sleepy Grace, Hope and Sinclair had made the half-hour trip home in silence. She'd asked him to drop her off at her car, which she'd left in the church parking lot, instead of driving her straight home, and he'd done that without question.

"Come in the house. Your mother's worried sick." Her father got out of the car and waited for her to do the same.

Hope's rubbery legs barely supported her, but her dad was right there, helping her make it up the porch steps. Deep lines of concern etched into the sides of his mouth, but thankfully he didn't ask again what she'd done that was so terrible.

She didn't want to tell him.

Not until she told Sinclair.

She chewed her bottom lip. Not tonight, though. What she'd done required a face-to-face confession. She'd tell him in the morning.

"Oh, honey." Her mom met them at the door and wrapped her arms around Hope.

Exhaustion from the emotional day took over, and Hope sobbed. Crying for everything she'd lost—her sister, her preschool and her future with Sinclair.

The next morning, Chuck Stillwell's barely contained annoyance filled Sinclair's small office. The guy wouldn't sit down, so Sinclair remained standing, too. "You wanted to meet first thing, so what's up?"

Chuck snorted. "Like you don't know."

"Humor me," Sinclair said through clenched teeth. He was in no mood to play guessing games.

"I don't appreciate my *pastor* sending his girlfriend to beg for money."

Sinclair tilted his head. "How's that?"

"Hope stopped by the farm last night, pleading *your* case for the preschool."

So that's where she'd gone. He thought the little girl's accident had stirred up painful memories about Sara's death. Hope had been distant on the ride home from the hospital, but Sinclair had thought she'd wanted space to grieve. So he'd dropped her off at her car like she'd asked and left her alone. Bad move on his part.

"Did she ask you to cover the transposed pledge?" It didn't sit well, but he had to know.

Obviously Hope didn't trust him enough, or she didn't trust God enough to see this thing through. He didn't know which was worse.

"In a matter of speaking, yes, she did. And I won't support a pastor who can't do his own dirty work. You got me?"

Sinclair flared his nostrils at the insult and the threat. "Do what you have to, Chuck. I'd never send Hope to you for money or anything else, but I won't apologize for her. She was broken up over the Cavanaugh girl's accident and did what she thought was right at the time."

"That's convenient. I suppose I have to believe that."

Sinclair leaned forward, wanting to cuff the guy, but he kept his fists firmly planted on the desktop and stared Chuck down instead. "Believe whatever makes you happy. While you're at it, find another church that'll make you happy. This preschool belongs to God, and He'll provide what we need with or without you."

Chuck's face registered surprise, and then a dash of respect crept in.

He'd called the guy's bluff without losing his temper, but Sinclair's satisfaction in finally putting Chuck Stillwell in his place was short-lived. He spotted Hope's father entering the main office like a hurricane about to make landfall. Jim Petersen looked more than a little upset.

"Excuse me." Sinclair's insides churned.

"We're not done here," Chuck warned.

"Yeah, we are." Sinclair left the guy sputtering behind him and rushed toward Hope's dad. "Mr. Petersen, is something wrong?"

Jim's eyes had an intimidating edge to them. No taller than Sinclair, Hope's father was broad enough to take anyone down a peg or two. And he looked mad enough to throw his weight around. "I was hoping you could tell me why my daughter cried herself to sleep last night."

Balling his hands into fists, Sinclair turned in time to catch Chuck's sheepish expression. "What did you say to her?"

"Whoa—wait a minute, I'm not the one on trial here."

Sinclair took a deep breath in an attempt to cool his temper and keep from saying something he'd regret later. He ground out, "You are now."

Jim Petersen stepped between them. "Would someone please tell me what's going on?"

Hope pumped gas into her car and stared at the gauges as they twirled from two to ten gallons. She could resign.

Once she told Sinclair what she'd done, she might have to.

Chuck Stillwell gave to the church regularly. His tithe checks collected in the offering plate every two weeks were huge. Without his financial support, cutbacks would have to be made. It only stood to reason that her salary would be one of them.

She pursed her lips as the gas pump clicked off with a clunk. Tank full, but she ran on fumes. After a sleepless night, her heart twisted every time she thought about Sinclair's reaction. This morning, she'd tell him what she'd done. She'd confess to going behind his back and doing exactly what he'd told her not to do. Even if he forgave her, would he ever trust her again?

Probably not.

She slammed the gas nozzle back into the pump's holster and marched toward the convenience store to pay. There had to be a way to fix this—but she'd done enough damage.

Inside the store, Hope's attention was caught by the donut case. She could wallow with a custard-filled Long John and coffee on her way to the office. It would most likely be her last day.

Perusing the tempting donuts, Hope nearly bumped into a woman. "Excuse me, I'm sorry."

"Miss Hope! *Hola,* good morning to you." Bonita Sanchez smiled.

"Hola."

"You sad, no?"

Hope smiled. She was worse than sad. Resigned,

deflated and sorrier than she'd ever been all fit the bill. "I'm tired, Bonita. I didn't sleep well."

"Discúlpame. I so sorry. My kids glad for Sunday school. You teach?"

Hope bit her lip. Maybe. If she still had a job, and Sinclair didn't send her packing. "I think so."

"My kids wait in car. I see you Sunday." Bonita smiled and hurried on her way.

"Adiós." Hope returned a smile she didn't feel and then focused her attention back on scanning the pastries.

She heard the tinkling sound of the bell on the store's glass door as Bonita left. An idea whispered through Hope's brain and warmed her heart.

What if...

Of course! Heart pumping, Hope dashed out of the convenience mart and spotted Bonita's old clunker of a car. She rushed forward and tapped on the hood to get the woman's attention. Her kids stuck their heads out of the lowered windows and waved, calling out her name.

Hope waved and, nearly breathless, asked, "Who watches your children while you work at Stillwell Farms?"

Bonita looked confused.

Hope repeated the question more slowly, in Spanish.

Bonita answered in Spanish, "One of the older

girls, most times. But sometimes we ladies take turns staying behind from the field."

"Thank you. Thank you so much." Hope backed away from her car and smiled.

Was it possible to incorporate a bilingual class into the summer program? Could she make it work? Would it make a difference in Chuck's decision?

Would it make a difference to Sinclair? This time, she'd check with him before acting on impulse. Even if Sinclair didn't forgive her for what she'd done, he'd recognize a good idea when he heard it. She owed him that much. It was worth a try.

Hope quickly paid the cashier and then headed for the church, her self-pity donuts forgotten. She prayed the whole way that God might take her colossal bungle and turn it around. She prayed that Sinclair would give her another shot, once he heard her apology and her promise to be up front with him in the future.

If they had one.

If he loved her…

Pulling into the church parking lot, Hope's stomach tightened when she saw Sinclair's Camaro parked beside a big white truck with the Stillwell Farms logo painted on its doors.

She bit her bottom lip.

She should have called him last night and saved

him from getting blindsided this morning. Dread settled even deeper when she spotted Judy's car in the parking lot. And why was her father's pickup here, too?

Hope got out of her car and squared her shoulders. She marched forward, prepared to face the consequences of her actions. But the closer she got to the office, the louder the unfamiliar sound of heated voices rang. With a hand to her belly to calm the turmoil there, Hope listened. She heard her name mentioned, but the rest remained unclear and muffled.

They really were going to fire her!

Her eyes stung and the back of her throat burned. It's what she deserved. She opened the door and went inside, prepared for the worst.

"You had no right to talk to Hope like that! She believed she owed you the truth." Sinclair looked furious.

Hope blinked. He was defending her?

Tension hung in the air as four people stood in the middle of the church office arguing. No one had heard her come inside.

"I thought you'd sent her!" Chuck's arms were spread wide in surrender or defense. Hope couldn't really tell, but there was a definite gleam in the man's eye, like he enjoyed the ruckus.

Her father rubbed his chin like he always did when gathering his thoughts. "Chuck, you know my daughter better than that. She wouldn't ask for anything unless there was an urgent need."

"If you'd all sit down, maybe we could iron this out civilly." Judy's voice of reason sounded firm, but she was ignored as the three men chorused their grievances.

Hope almost smiled at the scene before her. Almost.

"Chuck has every right to be offended." Hope spoke loudly enough to make her presence known.

All heads turned toward her.

"I was way out of line, and I'm sorry."

Sinclair's expression was hard to read, but he stepped toward her. "Hope—"

She held up her hand for him to wait. She needed to get this out, before he said the words that would break her heart. "I'm so sorry, Sinclair. I did what you told me not to do, and I hope you'll forgive me for not trusting you. For rushing ahead like a fool."

She took another step into the office. "And, Chuck, I beg your pardon for asking you to cover my mistake. That was wrong, but—"

She glanced at her father, who nodded for her to go on.

"Yes?" Judy prodded to cover the heavy pause.

And Sinclair smiled. He didn't look mad at her at all. He gestured for her to take the floor and run with it without hesitation or interruption. He trusted her.

Her courage bolstered by that small movement, Hope vowed she'd never again mess with his trust. Sinclair had grown into a man whose judgment she could rest in. Had she only listened to him, had she waited, she wouldn't be in this situation.

But God could fix this. He'd given her the idea.

Swallowing hard, Hope continued, "I didn't trust God to provide for the preschool, I see that now. I thought I could make this happen on my own, because I believe so strongly in the need. We need that preschool to provide a safe summer program, and we need it now. After Hannah's accident, the urgency to fight for it took over, and I couldn't sit back and do nothing."

She took a deep breath, but the four of them were looking at her as if seeing her for the first time. Maybe she'd finally said what they needed to hear. She'd always held back and waited for someone else to lead the charge. Well, maybe God wanted her to step up and lead for a change. She had the fire and vision for the preschool. Couldn't she help spread it?

"Despite going about it the wrong way, I'm more convinced than ever that we need the preschool." She looked at Chuck. "What if we offered a Spanish program during the summer, as well?

We might help your workers' kids, as well as others, learn English. It would help their parents, too."

When she saw the idea resonate in Chuck's eyes, she continued, "Wouldn't that be incentive for your migrant families to return every summer and give you a more effective workforce? Think of the opportunities we'd open up for those kids."

Chuck looked more than thoughtful. He looked convinced.

She peeked at Sinclair and loosened the iron-clad grip she had on the handle of her purse. She'd never seen him look at her with such pride before. And something else shone from his eyes, too, something so sweet it made her insides turn over.

It made her hope.

"Come on, Chuck. Vote for the preschool. You backed it before as the right choice. Why change when the need is so evident?" her father asked.

Sinclair stepped toward Chuck and held out his hand in peace. "You once said to me that you'd only give to missions that impacted *your* community. I can't think of a better mission field then your workers' kids and kids like Hannah in this community."

There was no doubting Sinclair's conviction was real this time. His voice carried a hint of steel, too. He'd help lead the charge until everyone was on board. They both would. They'd do this together.

Hope held her breath in an attempt to quiet her wildly beating heart.

"Listen to them," Judy added. "It's tax deductible, for pity's sake."

Chuck laughed at that, and then he took Sinclair's hand for a mighty shake. "Okay, okay, but I'm sticking with my original pledge." He gave her a quick wink. "The correct one."

Hope let out her breath in a whoosh and then laughed. Maybe God wanted to test her trust in Him for the rest. It didn't matter. As long as they remained united as a church behind the preschool, they'd find a way.

"Hope, we need to check out if there's any state funding available for a bilingual program." The excitement in Sinclair's voice was contagious.

"I'll check on that today." Hope's head spun with the possibilities. Considering the agricultural nature of the area, there had to be something out there for them.

They'd find a way.

"Then we are agreed to uphold our last vote to move forward." Judy clapped her hands together once in resolution like they'd broken from a sports huddle. "I'll schedule a meeting next week so we can update everyone with the new direction. I'll help Hope get our financing application updated, and once the pledges are made, we'll break ground."

Sinclair took hold of Hope's hand. "We'll renew the pledge drive this Sunday. I've already got a call into the builder we met yesterday to see what kind of estimate he can give us." Then he threaded his fingers through hers. "This is going to work."

"Thank you." She tugged Sinclair close for a hug, her heart full.

His arms tightened around her.

"Hey, hey. Haven't you two learned anything from the Cherry Festival?" Chuck thumbed toward the door, but his grin teased. "Take it outside."

Hope pulled back and giggled like a teenager. Glancing at Sinclair, she noticed the nod he exchanged with her father. What was that all about?

Then he pulled her toward the door. "You heard the man. Let's take this outside."

Again she laughed and nearly tripped trying to keep up with Sinclair. She felt a little light-headed, along with a shiver of anticipation.

Once outside, Sinclair lifted her into his arms and spun her around. "This is finally coming together, sweetheart. Thanks to you."

His endearment made her heart sing. She liked being his sweetheart, but she wanted to be more. So much more. She prayed he'd want that, too.

When he put her back on her feet, she looked into his eyes. "I almost ruined everything. I'm so sorry I went to Chuck when you told me not to."

He tucked her hair behind her ears. "I know why you did it. Your heart was in the right place, but my pride got in the way. I needed to let that go. I think Chuck and I understand each other better now, and I've got you to thank for that."

Hope laughed. "That's one way of putting it."

He touched his nose to hers. "He likes saving the day."

"Yeah, I think you're right."

"Enough talk about Chuck." Sinclair's eyes grew serious as he took both her hands in his. "Hope, I know we should date awhile, but I don't think that's going to work."

She searched his face and grinned. "You're right, it's not."

At the surprised look on his face, she continued, "I think I've waited long enough to tell you that I love you."

He wrapped her arms around his neck and pulled her close. "Then what do you propose we do about it?"

Hope took a deep breath. "Get married."

"When?" Sinclair brushed his lips against hers.

Hope tried to think clearly. How long would it take to plan a backyard wedding? "How about when your house is ready?"

"Our house. I bought it for us."

Her eyes widened. "Really? You never said so."

"How could I? I've been trying to do this right

and not rush things, and here you are proposing to me after only two dates."

She shook her head. "I've loved you since I was fifteen. That's not exactly rushing things."

He chuckled and cupped her face for another soft kiss. "And I love you, Hope Petersen. It just took me longer to figure that out."

Hope nearly burst with happiness. "When did you know?"

"For certain? When you fell down at the Fourth of July picnic. But I had a pretty good hint the moment I begged you not to quit."

"I'm so glad that I didn't," Hope whispered.

"Me, too." He gave her another featherlight kiss. "I need you in so many ways. You're part of who I am."

"You're part of who I've become," Hope said.

"I love who you've become, but you're supposed to let me do the asking."

She grinned. "Well, get to it then."

"Bossy girl. Will you marry me?"

"Absolutely."

He kissed her then, thoroughly and with such tenderness that her entire body melted into him.

She felt like they'd joined their souls at last. And it was well worth the wait.

Epilogue

Three weeks later, Hope looped her arm through her father's and they stepped off the porch of the house where she'd grown up. She'd experienced so much heartache here, and finally she'd leave home wrapped in joy.

"Ready?" her dad asked.

She scanned the throng of wedding guests. Chuck and Mary Stillwell sat on her side toward the front, as if they were her family. They were. They were part of her church family.

Chuck had given Sinclair the keys to the Stillwell family's summer cottage on Mackinac Island for their honeymoon. After spending their wedding night in their own house, they'd make the trip there for a nice long week of fun.

Her gaze rested on Sinclair, who stood tall and handsome in a light tan suit fixed with a black-eyed Susan wildflower pinned to his lapel. He stood alone, next to her church's previous minister, who'd traveled north to marry them.

Sinclair smiled when he saw her.

She smiled in return. "Yeah, I'm ready."

"I hope Sinclair knows what a beautiful woman he's getting for a wife," her father said.

She patted his arm. "Thanks, Dad, but he knows."

Hope had dressed in a simple white eyelet gown that brushed her ankles. Her hair had been scattered with wildflowers that echoed her bouquet of black-eyed Susans and sweet pea.

"Watch your step," her dad whispered as they slowly made their way across the gravel driveway. "Don't know why you wouldn't wear shoes."

"I don't need them." Hope had once told her sister, during Sara's fuss over shoes for her wedding with Ryan, that she wouldn't care if she married barefoot. As long as she married the man she loved, she'd be happy.

That man had always been Sinclair.

Hope believed Sara looked down on them today, and she probably laughed at Hope's bare feet, but it sent a message. One her sister would appreciate.

She spotted Ryan in the front row, sitting with his family on the groom's side, looking solemn but pleased. Hope understood why he'd gently refused Sinclair's offer to stand in as best man. Sara would have been her matron of honor, and no one could adequately fill that role. So no one did.

Hope offered up a quick prayer for her new brother-in-law, asking God to heal his heart and bring him peace—and one day, maybe even bring him new love.

* * * * *

If you enjoyed this story by Jenna Mindel, be sure to check out the other books this month from Love Inspired!

Dear Reader,

Thank you so much for picking up a copy of my book. I hope you've enjoyed the characters as much as I have. I had no intention of writing a minister hero, but Sinclair Marsh, a mere mention in *Season of Dreams* (February 2011), had a mind of his own and he pretty much steamrolled his way into my brain. The surprise came when this book turned out to be Hope's story about her pain in loving Sinclair for so many years—her first love, who'd always wandered away from her.

Makes me wonder how hurt God feels when His people wander away from His steadfast love. Thank goodness that real love is always there for us, and no matter how far we wander, forgiveness is one turn around, where we can come home to the blessed arms of Jesus, God's only son.

Many blessings,
Jenna

I'd love to hear from you. Please visit my website at www.jennamindel.com or drop me a note c/o Love Inspired Books, 233 Broadway, Suite 1001, New York, NY 10279

Questions for Discussion

1. *Courting Hope* opens with Hope Petersen threatening to quit her job. Is she justified in that reaction? How would you feel if you were in her shoes?

2. Sinclair Marsh has returned home after three years of running away from his part in an accident that killed Hope's sister. Saying he's sorry doesn't quite cut it when he approaches Hope's parents. Was he right to apologize so early in the book, or should he have waited until after he'd rebuilt the relationship? Why or why not?

3. Hope's feelings for Sinclair resurface, and that frustrates her to no end. She's always loved him, yet considering that her feelings were never returned, why couldn't she get over her first love? Do you believe love is something that just hits you, or is it a choice?

4. Do you remember your first love with fondness or despair?

5. Hope is surprised to find out that her father's issue with Sinclair is about her, not about her

sister's accident. Why is Hope's dad trying so hard to protect her? Is he right to do so?

6. Sinclair's brother, Ryan, is bitter over how long Sinclair has been away. Why is it so hard to forgive the ones we love when they let us down?

7. Hope tends to think of others before herself. An admirable trait, but how has that held her back from realizing her own dreams? Is there something you'd like to do but you're holding back for fear of letting someone else down?

8. Sinclair wants to court Hope, but decides that he should first overcome the obstacles that might stand in their way. One of those hurdles is getting approval from Hope's parents before asking her out. Should he have worried about that? Why or why not?

9. Sinclair battles an impulsive nature that has gotten him and Hope into trouble in the past. How does Sinclair show that he's grown out of that throughout the story?

10. We don't always know why we have to wait for things, but God knows, and we can trust that He knows what is best for us. God brought Sinclair home at the right time for him to fall

in love with Hope and fulfill her heart's desire. Does waiting make the receiving any sweeter? Why or why not?

11. The bible verse I chose for *Courting Hope* is Ecclesiastes 3: there is a time for everything under heaven. Take a moment and read the entire chapter of Ecclesiastes 3. How do you interpret that passage?

LARGER-PRINT BOOKS!

GET 2 FREE
LARGER-PRINT NOVELS
PLUS 2 FREE
MYSTERY GIFTS

Love Inspired

Larger-print novels are now available...

LARGER-PRINT BOOKS!

GET 2 FREE LARGER-PRINT NOVELS PLUS 2 FREE MYSTERY GIFTS

Love Inspired®
SUSPENSE
RIVETING INSPIRATIONAL ROMANCE

Larger-print novels are now available...

YES! Please send me 2 FREE LARGER-PRINT Love Inspired® Suspense novels and my 2 FREE mystery gifts (gifts are worth about $10). After receiving them, if I don't wish to receive any more books, I can return the shipping statement marked "cancel." If I don't cancel, I will receive 4 brand-new novels every month and be billed just $5.24 per book in the U.S. or $5.74 per book in Canada. That's a savings of at least 23% off the cover price. It's quite a bargain! Shipping and handling is just 50¢ per book in the U.S. and 75¢ per book in Canada.* I understand that accepting the 2 free books and gifts places me under no obligation to buy anything. I can always return a shipment and cancel at any time. Even if I never buy another book, the two free books and gifts are mine to keep forever.

110/310 IDN F5CC

Name _____
(PLEASE PRINT)

Address _____ Apt. #

City _____ State/Prov. _____ Zip/Postal Code

Signature (if under 18, a parent or guardian must sign)

Mail to the Harlequin® Reader Service:
IN U.S.A.: P.O. Box 1867, Buffalo, NY 14240-1867
IN CANADA: P.O. Box 609, Fort Erie, Ontario L2A 5X3

Are you a current subscriber to Love Inspired Suspense books and want to receive the larger-print edition?
Call 1-800-873-8635 or visit www.ReaderService.com.

* Terms and prices subject to change without notice. Prices do not include applicable taxes. Sales tax applicable in N.Y. Canadian residents will be charged applicable taxes. Offer not valid in Quebec. This offer is limited to one order per household. Not valid for current subscribers to Love Inspired Suspense larger-print books. All orders subject to credit approval. Credit or debit balances in a customer's account(s) may be offset by any other outstanding balance owed by or to the customer. Please allow 4 to 6 weeks for delivery. Offer available while quantities last.

Your Privacy—The Harlequin® Reader Service is committed to protecting your privacy. Our Privacy Policy is available online at www.ReaderService.com or upon request from the Harlequin Reader Service.

We make a portion of our mailing list available to reputable third parties that offer products we believe may interest you. If you prefer that we not exchange your name with third parties, or if you wish to clarify or modify your communication preferences, please visit us at www.ReaderService.com/consumerschoice or write to us at Harlequin Reader Service Preference Service, P.O. Box 9062, Buffalo, NY 14269. Include your complete name and address.

LISLPDIR13R

ReaderService.com

Manage your account online!

- Review your order history
- Manage your payments
- Update your address

> *We've designed
> the Harlequin® Reader Service
> website just for you.*

Enjoy all the features!

- Reader excerpts from any series
- Respond to mailings and special monthly offers
- Discover new series available to you
- Browse the Bonus Bucks catalog
- Share your feedback

Visit us at:

ReaderService.com